英國入籍試 解題天書

LIFE IN THE
UK TEST

英國入籍試 1 Take Pass

Life in the UK Test，一般被稱為「英國入籍試」，這考試對於想長期居留英國人士非常重要。

因為無論你是持有以下何種簽證：BNO5+1、居英權二代、配偶簽證、投資移民簽證、企業家簽證、海外公司首席代表簽證、創新者簽證、工作簽證等，都必須通過 Life in the UK Test，才可以申請英國永久居留權，有英國永久居留權，才可以申請入籍英國，由此可見 Life in the UK Test 的重要性。

應試者必須在 45 分鐘內，回答 24 條選擇題，當中需要 18 條答對。而最重要的是，試題的內容結合了當地的歷史、文化、政經、傳統習俗、法律和政治制度等多個範疇，例如：

* 哪位作曲家曾為喬治一世和喬治二世作曲？
* 1944 年的《教育法》為英國帶來了什麼？
* 哪些行業在大蕭條時期乘勢而興？
* 英國於哪一年廢除奴隸制度

這些問題對於本地人來說，也未必有把握可以取得滿分，更何況是外來移民？有國際知名通訊社曾隨機調查了 40 名英國當地人，只有一半人可以悉數答對，足見程度之艱深。

本書就是希望通過數百條熱門題目反覆測試、不斷操練，而且輔以中英對照，加上詳細題解，幫助準備申請永居及入籍英國的讀者，輕鬆搞定「入籍英國試」，讓大家都可以「1 Take Pass」。

Koo Sir 前作《入籍英國考試全攻略 Life in the UK Test》已經幫助不少有志者成功通過考試，現再接再厲出版本書，全新題庫，解讀更清晰易明，目的是希望更多香港人無痛 pass，並且能更了解英國歷史政經，以及社會文化，盡快融入本地生活。

心願，自信定能圓

六年前，總覺得路很長，但二零二二年五月某天，終於也來到 Citizenship Ceremony 宣誓成為英國公民的這天，同一時間有二十個朋友，來自十多個不同國家及地區，我是惟一 Hongkonger。「天佑女皇」音樂響起的一刻，我閉上眼回想到登上往英國單程航班的那天，彷彿也只是昨日。

但這天的到來，又要倒數回到二零二零年九月某天，應考的Life in the UK test，也是以往俗稱的「英國入籍試」，現在大部分的英國簽證，在第五年向英國 home office 申請永久居留前，都必須要通過 Life in the UK test，有了永久居留權的一年後，才能申請 Citizenship，審批後，才能正式入籍英國。

所以宣誓入籍的這天，前提是必須要通過Life in the UK test，取得永久居留權，可見這考試的重要性。

朋友問：「我的英文不好，Life in the UK test 難嗎？」我的回應是：只要平日多留意英國生活的日常和本地新聞，用心多做練習，應該不難應付吧。

我在應考前都用了不少時間，反覆做了很多練習，不懂的，尤其是深度歷史題和文化題比較難應付，我都會上網再找中文資料，理解後更易明白。

本書的題目和解題都是中英對照，讓準備應試者更易理解和掌握題目的內容，易懂易記，而且模擬試題部份像真度極高，多加練習，相信合格甚至一次就成功的機會很大呢。

祝大家都心願達成，安居樂業。

fb「香港人在英國專頁」版主　黎瑋思 fb@HongKongerInUK

目錄

序/ 英國入籍試 1 Take Pass   2

推薦序 / 心願，自信定能圓 / 黎瑋思 香港人在英國 fb 版主   4

Chapter 1
關於英國入籍試 Life in the UK Test   9

01. 什麼是英國入籍試？/02. 為什麼你一定要通過英國入籍試？
/03. 如何通過考試？/04. 我需要如何學習？/05. 何時可以應考？
有效期有多久？/06. 怎樣預約考期？要到哪裡應試？/07. 考試費
用多少？/08. 考試當天的程序？/09. 考試完成，結果通知/10. 假如
考試不及格/11. 入籍儀式/12. 入籍儀式舉行當日，會有什麼安排？

Chapter 2
題庫練習 Practice Questions

2.1 單選題（四選一）Select one correct answer from four options   18

    單選題（答案）Answer   43

2.2 正誤判斷題 Decide whether a statement is true or false   56

    正誤判斷題（答案）Answer   74

2.3 正確項選擇（二選一）Select the statement which you think is correct   85

    正確項選擇（答案）Answer   109

2.4 多選題（四選二）Select two correct answers from four options   120

    多選題（答案）Answer   139

Chapter 3
模擬試卷Mock Papers

3.1 模擬試卷一 Paper 1 question   150

模擬試卷一（答案）Answer   157

3.2 模擬試卷二 Paper 2 question   161

模擬試卷二（答案）Answer   167

3.3 模擬試卷三 Paper 3 question   171

模擬試卷三（答案）Answer   177

3.4 模擬試卷四 Paper 4 question   181

模擬試卷四（答案）Answer   189

3.5 模擬試卷五 Paper 5 question   194

模擬試卷五（答案）Answer   201

Chapter 4
常見問題

205

Chapter 1
關於英國入籍試
Life in the UK Test

01. 什麼是英國入籍試？

Life in the UK Test（一般被稱為「英國入籍試」）是一個由英國內政部於 2005 年推出，對於申請歸化入籍之非歐盟人士的英語語言和英國生活基本知識測試， 2007 年更延伸到「永居申請」（Indefinite Leave to Remain，或 ILR），並於 2013 年起成為所有永居和入籍申請者所必須通過之考試。

無論你是持有以下何種簽證：BNO 5+1、居英權二代 British Citizen by Descent、配偶簽證 Spouse Visa、投資額簽證 Investor Visa、企業家簽證 Tier1 Entrepreneur Visa、海外公司首席代表簽證 Sole Representative Visa、 創新者簽證 Innovator Visa、 工作簽證 Tier 2 General Work Visa 等，都必須通過 Life in the UK Test，才可以申請永久居留權。（除非申請人的年齡是 18 歲以下或 65 歲以上，方可獲豁免。）

02. 為什麼你一定要通過英國入籍試？

Life in the UK Test 是非常實用的英語語言和英國生活基本知識考核，從 2013 年起申請英國永居和入籍的所有人必須通過這一考試， 否則將功虧一簣，無法拿到永居簽證或入籍。

03. 如何通過考試？

Life in the UK Test 考試結構簡單，全卷只有 24 道題目，內含單選題、多選題、正誤判斷題、正確項選擇題，共4類。

考生只要在 45 分鐘內最少做對其中 18 道題（正確率最少達 75%）就可以通過考試。所以，通過有效地指導，針對性的培訓，達到一定量的訓練，絕對可以通過考試。

i. 考試形式

英國生活測試包括 24 個有關今日英國生活重要方面的問題。你將在電腦上進行測試，並在 45 分鐘內完成所有問題。為了通過測試，你必須正確回答 18 個問題。這些問題基於英國生活的各個方面。

ii. 題目類型

題目分 4 類：

a. 單選題：從 4 個選項中選擇一個正確答案。以下是示例：

Question: Which is the most popular sport in the UK?

A. Football

B. Rugby

C. Golf

D. Tennis

b. 正誤判斷題：確定陳述句是對還是錯。以下是示例：

Question: Is the statement below TRUE or FALSE?

The daffodil is the national flower of Wales.

A. True

B. False

c. 正確項選擇題：從 **2** 個陳述中選擇一個你認為正確的陳述。以下是示例：

1. Which of the following statements is correct?

A. Shakespeare wrote 'To be or not to be'.

B. Shakespeare wrote 'We will fight them on the beaches'.

d. 多選題：從 **4** 個選項中揀 **2** 個正確答案。以下是示例：

Question: Which TWO political parties formed the coalition government in 2010? (Choose TWO)

A. Conservatives

B. Labor

C. Communists

D. Liberal Democrats

04. 我需要如何學習？

要通過 **Life in the UK Test**，你需要閱讀《**Life in the United Kingdom: A Guide for New Residents**》。這些章節涵蓋了作為英國永久居民或公民需要了解的一系列主題：

- 英國的價值觀和原則

- 組成英國的國家

- 塑造了我們歷史的事件和人物
- 英國生活的方方面面
- 我們的國家是如何治理的
- 你如何參與你的社區

05. 何時可以應考？有效期有多久？

抵達英國安頓好後就可以報考 Life in the UK test，一經合格，終生有效。

06. 怎樣預約考期？要到哪裡應試？

你可以到 lifeintheuktest.gov.uk 排期預約考試。英國有超過 35 個考場。當你在網上預約考期時，你會獲得最近你試場的詳細資料。

07. 考試費用多少？

考試費用為 50 英鎊。

08. 考試當天的程序？

當你到達試場時，你需要向監考人員出示在你註冊時使用的身份證件，並顯示你郵政編碼證明的文件。

如沒有攜帶上述文件，你將無法參加考試。

工作人員會檢查你的文件，經核實後，你的隨身物品及手提電話等必須放入儲物櫃，不能帶入試場。

然後會進入試場，你將可以登入電腦，準備考試。

正式考試前，會有一個電腦練習（旨在供考生練習使用滑鼠及利用鼠標作答）。測試結果並不會影響你在正式考試的最終分數。

當準備好後，考官會告訴你何時可以開始作答，你將有 45 分鐘的時間進行測試，考生會用電腦作答。場內亦會提供耳機供閣下收聽問題和答案選項之用。

在此期間，你將不能翻閱書本或筆記，也不能使用任何電子器材（例如手提電話、藍芽耳機或電腦）。一經發現，閣下的考試資格將被取消。

09. 考試完成，結果通知

以往假如成功通過考試，考官會即時發一封你必須簽字

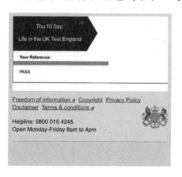

的「通過通知信」（Pass Notification Letter），信內會寫有你的考試日期、試場主任、中心位置和獨特的ID 編號等詳細信息。

疫情期間，已將以上程序更改，考生完成考試後，取回個人物品就必須離開試場，一會兒後會收到電郵通知。

記緊將「通過通知信」的電郵好好保存，因為當閣下申請永久居留權或公民時，你必須要填上電郵內代表你通過Life in the UK test 的一組號碼，因此妥善保管它非常重要。

10. **假如考試不及格**

假如未能通過考試，同樣會收到一封結果通知信。你將需要再次參加考試，並重新預約及繳付考試費用。你必須等至少 7 天，才能再次應考。

參加考試的次數不限。在你通過考試之前，你不能申請永久居留及申請成為英國公民。

11. **入籍儀式**

如果你的公民身份申請成功，內政部將向你發送一封確認信，並邀請你參加「入籍儀式」（Citizenship ceremony）。儀式通常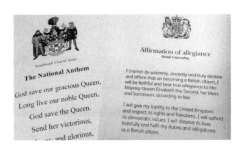會在你居住的地方附近舉行。（假如你想儀式在英國其他地方舉行，則需早在申請入籍時提出要求。）

當你收到入籍儀式的邀請，你會有 90 天的時間參加。一般而言，你可以帶同兩位客人一起參與。出席儀式僅限受邀參加。

如你想安排私人儀式，那你應該與你的地方當局討論這個問題。你可能需要因而支付額外費用。

當你參加你的儀式時，你必須宣誓效忠（Citizenship Oath）和宣讀誓言，這些是你成為英國公民必須作出的承諾。

12. 入籍儀式舉行當日，會有什麼安排？

當到達儀式現場時，工作人員會檢查你的身份，並確認你證書上的個人信息是否屬實。

在儀式上，通常由重要的地方或國家人士發表演講。其中可能包括代表當地歡迎新公民，並鼓勵他們在社區中發揮積極作用。

你將獲得英國公民證書和歡迎禮包。有時，新公民更會收到議會的小禮物。在演奏國歌時，所有新公民都被邀請起立。

一些地方當局安排拍攝事件的照片或進行攝錄。如果你願意，你可以購回這些相片或錄像。

Chapter 2
題　庫　練　習
Practice Questions

1. **Which country invented rugby?**

    欖球起源於哪個國家?

    A. India 印度

    B. Argentina 阿根廷

    C. England 英國

    D. France 法國

2. **Where did the Huguenots migrate from?**

    胡格諾派是來自哪個國家?

    A. France 法國

    B. Italy 意大利

    C. Pakistan 巴基斯坦

    D. Cyprus 塞浦路斯

3. **Where is the Northern Ireland Assembly located?**

    北愛爾蘭議會大廈位於哪個城市?

    A. London 倫敦

    B. Belfas 貝爾法斯特

    C. Cardiff 卡迪夫

    D. Dublin 都柏林

4. **Which of the following British scientists showed how gravity applied to the whole universe?**

哪位英國科學家將引力概念，應用到宇宙之上？

A. Alan Turing　亞倫‧杜林

B. Alexander Fleming　亞歷山大‧弗萊明

C. Isaac Newton　艾薩克‧牛頓

D. Ernest Rutherford　歐內斯特‧盧瑟福

5. **Which composer wrote music for King George I and II?**

哪位作曲家曾為喬治一世和喬治二世作曲？

A. George Frederick Handel　喬治‧弗雷德里克‧亨德爾

B. Gustav Holst　古斯塔夫‧霍爾斯特

C. Ralph Vaughan Williams　拉爾夫‧沃恩‧威廉姆斯

D. Henry Purcell　亨利‧珀塞爾

6. **When was the English Civil War broke out?**

英國內戰始於哪一年？

A. 1632

B. 1635

C. 1642

D. 1652

7. **Which British landmark was built as part of the UK's celebration of the new millenium?**

    以下哪個地標是為慶祝英國踏入新千禧年而建？

    A. London Bridge 倫敦橋

    B. Tower Bridge 倫敦塔橋

    C. Westminster Abbey 威斯敏斯特教堂

    D. The London Eye 倫敦眼

8. **What type of government does the UK have?**

    英國是什麼類型政府？

    A. Dictatorship 獨裁政府

    B. Federal government 聯邦政府

    C. Parliamentary democracy 議會民主政體

    D. Communist government 共產主義

9. **What was the Spanish Armada?**

    什麼是「西班牙無敵艦隊」？

    A. A large fleet of planes 龐大的飛機部隊

    B. A group of radicals 一群激進分子

    C. A group of politicians 一群政客

    D. A large fleet of ships 龐大的艦隊

10. **Who defeated the English at the Battle of Bannockburn in 1314?**

    誰在 1314 年爆發的班諾克本戰役中，擊敗英國？

    A. Robert the Bruce　羅拔・布魯士

    B. King Edward I　英王愛德華一世

    C. Admiral Nelson　納爾遜海軍上將

    D. The Normans　諾曼人

11. **Prince Philip is also known as:**

    菲臘親王又名為：

    A. The Duke of Wellington　威靈頓公爵

    B. The Prince of Wales　威爾斯親王

    C. The Duke of Edinburgh　愛丁堡公爵

    D. The Prince of Northern Ireland　北愛爾蘭親王

12. **Where is the Millennium Stadium?**

    千禧球場在以下哪個地方？

    A. Birmingham　伯明翰

    B. Nottingham　諾定咸

    C. Liverpool　利物浦

    D. Cardiff　卡迪夫

13. **Who lost a lot of their power after the Battle of Culloden in 1746?**

卡洛登戰役在 1746 年結束後，誰大大地失去了權力和影響力？

A. The Church　教會

B. Politicians　政治家

C. The Clans　氏族

D. The Queen　女王

14. **Which UK landmark was elected as 'Britain's favorite view' in 2007?**

英國哪個地標在 2007 年被評為「英國最受歡迎景觀」？

A. Wastwater in the Lake District

英國湖區內的沃斯特湖

B. Snowdon in Snowdonia

史諾多尼亞入面的斯諾登山

C. The Crown Jewels at the Tower of London

倫敦塔內的英國王權之物

D. Loch Lomond in Scotland

蘇格蘭的羅莽湖

15. **When did freedom of the press start?**

新聞自由於哪一年開始？

A. 1795

B. 1685

C. 1695

D. 1785

16. **What was the last successful foreign invasion of England?**

英格蘭最後一次成功入侵別國的戰役是什麼？

A. The Roman invasion　羅馬入侵

B. The Anglo - Saxon invasion　盎格魯 - 撒克遜入侵

C. The Norman Conquest　諾曼征服

D. The Viking invasion　維京入侵

17. **Who was Richard Austen Butler?**

李察•奧斯丁•畢拿是誰？

A. British economist　英國經濟學家

B. Welsh poet　威爾斯詩人

C. Labour MP　工黨議員

D. Conservative MP　保守黨國會議員

18. **Where was Isaac Newton from?**

哪裡是艾薩克•牛頓的出生地？

A. Lincolnshire　林肯郡

B. Stratford - upon - Avon　埃文河畔斯特拉特福

C. Cardiff　卡迪夫

D. Edinburgh　愛丁堡

19. **Under which Act was The Kingdom of Great Britain created?**

大不列顛王國是根據哪條法案或法令創建？

A. The Reform Act 1832　《1832 年改革法案》

B. The Act of Union 1707　《1707 年聯合法令》

C. The Emancipation Proclamation 1863　《1863年解放法案》

D. The Butler Act 1925　《1925 年巴特勒法案》

20. **Where is the National Horseracing Museum located?**

國家賽馬博物館在哪裡？

A. Newmarket　新市

B. New England　新英格蘭

C. Newcastle　紐卡素

D. New Jersey　新澤西

21. **Which of the following countries belongs to the European Union?**

以下哪個國家是歐盟成員？

A. Norway　挪威

B. Switzerland　瑞士

C. Croatia　克羅地亞

D. Algeria　阿爾及利亞

22. **What were the first Women's Social and Political Union Group (founded in 1903) members called?**

1903年成立的「婦女社會和政治聯盟」，其成員叫什麼名字？

A. Gentry　紳士

B. Boers　布爾斯

C. Rebels　叛軍

D. Suffragettes　婦女參政運動者

23. **Where did the Boer War take place?**

布爾戰爭發生於哪個國家？

A. South Africa　南非

B. India　印度

C. Bangladesh　孟加拉

D. Mauritius　毛里裘斯

24. **Which year did the Battle of Agincourt break out?**

阿金庫爾戰役於哪一年爆發？

A. 1348

B. 1415

C. 1315

D. 1448

25. **What is the 'Bessemer process'?**

什麼是「貝塞麥過程」？

A. An industrial process for the mass production of iron

　　大規模生產鐵的工業過程

B. An industrial process for the mass production of copper

　　大規模生產銅的工業過程

C. An industrial process for the mass production of titanium

　　大規模生產鈦的工業過程

D. An industrial process for the mass production of steel

　　大規模生產鋼鐵的工業過程

26. **When did England win the World Cup?**

英格蘭於哪一年贏得世界盃冠軍？

A. 1974

B. 1986

C. 1982

D. 1966

27. **During the Battle of Trafalgar, Britain fought against which two countries?**

在「特拉法加海戰」中，英國與哪兩個國家打仗？

A. France and Belgium　法國、比利時

B. France and Spain　法國、西班牙

C. France and Italy　法國、意大利

D. Italy and Spain　意大利、西班牙

28. **What caused the Ireland famine in the middle of the 19th century?**

為什麼愛爾蘭在 19 世紀中鬧饑荒？

A. heat wave　熱浪侵襲

B. flooding　遇到洪水

C. crop failed　農作物失收

D. not enough farmers　農民數目不足

29. **What happened at the Battle of Britain?**

不列顛戰役（或英倫空戰）是一場怎樣的戰爭？

A. Naval battle against Spain 與西班牙的海戰

B. Aerial battle against France 與法國的空戰

C. Aerial battle against Germany 與德國的空戰

D. Naval battle against France 與法國的海戰

30. **Who selects the local Chief Constable?**

警察局長是由誰挑選？

A. Judge 法官

B. Police and Crime Commissioners 警察和犯罪專員

C. Mayor 市長

D. Local community members 本地社區成員

31. **How many British died on the first day alone of the Battle of the Somme?**

在索姆河戰役開戰首天，就有幾多英國人喪生？

A. 60,000

B. 65,000

C. 40,000

D. 55,000

32. **Which year was the first Union flag created?**

第一面「聯合旗」（即米字旗）在哪一年出現？

A. 1515

B. 1616

C. 1505

D. 1606

33. **Big Ben is the nickname for the great bell of the clock at _____ in London.**

大本鐘（或譯作大笨鐘）是倫敦哪個地點大鐘的暱稱。

A. London Eye　倫敦眼

B. Houses of Parliament　國會大樓

C. The Shard　碎片大廈

D. Sky Garden　空中花園

34. **Where was Anne Boleyn executed?**

安妮·博林在哪裡被處決？

A. Conwy Castle　康威城堡

B. The Tower of London　倫敦塔

C. The Houses of the Parliament　國會大廈

D. France　法國

35. **What do Sir Terence Conran, Clarice Cliff and Thomas Chippendale have in common?**

泰倫斯康蘭爵士、克拉瑞斯克里夫和湯瑪斯齊本德爾，有什麼共同點？

A. They were British designers　他們都是英國設計師

B. They developed the atomic bomb　他們研製了原子彈

C. They were British explorers　他們都是英國探險家

D. They were British poets　他們都是英國詩人

36. **Which of the following cities is not in Wales?**

以下哪個城市不在威爾斯？

A. Cardiff　卡迪夫

B. Swansea　史雲斯

C. Bradford　巴拉福特

D. Newport　紐波特

37. **Which Saxon king of England was killed at the Battle of Hastings in 1066?**

哪位撒克遜國王在 1066 年的「黑斯廷斯戰役」中陣亡？

A. Kenneth MacAlpin　肯尼斯·麥克阿爾派恩

B. Harold　哈羅德

C. William the Conqueror　「征服者威廉」威廉一世

D. Henry V　亨利五世

38. **How can one be protected from being forced into a marriage by the law?**

    法律如何保障個人免被迫婚？

    A. By giving them a place to stay away from their family 為對方安排一個能遠離家人的避難所

    B. Court orders can be obtained to protect a person from being forced into a marriage

    由法庭頒令，保護該人不會被迫婚。

    C. By speaking to the person's parents

    通過與該受害人的雙親交談

    D. There are no laws in the UK to avoid this

    沒有法律能避免這種事發生

39. **When did the BBC start the world's first regular TV broadcast?**

    英國廣播公司於哪一年提供全球首個常規電視服務？

    A. 1922

    B. 1932

    C. 1936

    D. 1944

40. The evacuation of British and French soldiers from France in a huge naval operation during World War II, gave rise to which term below?

在第二次世界大戰進行期間，英、法兩國士兵大規模從海路由法國撤離，該次軍事行動衍生出以下哪個名詞？

A. The Harbour Spirit　海港精神

B. The Blitz Operation　大轟炸精神

C. The Dunkirk Spirit　鄧寇克精神

D. The D - Day Operation　作戰日行動

41. Which programme below aims to help 16 and 17 year - olds develop their skills and become part in community projects?

下列哪個項目旨在幫助 16 和 17 歲的孩子培養技能，並參與地區項目？

A. the Youth Working programme　青年就業計劃

B. the National Development programme　國家發展計劃

C. the National Citizen Service programme

　　全國公民服務計劃

D. the Skills Development programme　技能發展計劃

42. When was Queen Victoria on the throne?

維多利亞女王於哪一年登上王位？

A. 1837

B. 1847

C. 1835

D. 1836

43. **Who wrote the books 'Pride and Prejudice' and 'Sense and Sensibility'?**

《傲慢與偏見》和《理智與情感》是誰的作品？

A. Charles Dickens　查理・狄更斯

B. Robert Louis Stevenson　羅拔・路易斯・史堤芬遜

C. Evelyn Waugh　伊芙蓮・沃

D. Jane Austen　珍・奧斯丁

44. **Why is 1928 an important year for women's rights?**

為什麼 1928 年對女權來說，是重要的一年？

A. Women could vote at 18, the same age as men.

　　凡年滿 18 歲的女性都可以投票，地位與男性相同。

B. Women could vote at 21, the same age as men.

　　凡年滿 21 歲的女性都可以投票，地位與男性相同。

C. Women could vote if they were over 30 years old.

　　年滿 30 歲以上的女性，都可以投票。

D. None of the above.　以上皆否

45. **Who designed the Dumfries House in Scotland?**

位於蘇格蘭的鄧弗里斯莊園是由哪位著名建築師設計？

A. Sir Christopher Wren　基斯杜化・雷恩爵士

B. Robert Adam　羅拔・亞當

C. Sir Norman Foster　諾曼・科士打爵士

D. Dame Zaha Hadid　扎哈・哈迪德夫人

46. **Which tribe(s) invaded Britain?**

    以下哪個部落曾入侵不列顛？

    A. The Jutes 朱特人

    B. The Angles 盎格魯人

    C. The Saxons 撒克遜人

    D. All of the above 以上皆是

47. **Where is the most famous sailing event in the UK held?**

    英國最著名的帆船賽事於哪裡舉行？

    A. Holyhead, North Wales 霍利黑德（威爾斯以北）

    B. Cowes, The Isle of Wight 考斯（懷特島）

    C. Douglas, The Isle of Man

    　道格拉斯（馬恩島，或稱曼島）

    D. Plymouth, England 普利茅夫（英格蘭）

48. **Which of the following is the British overseas territory located in the South Atlantic?**

    以下哪個地方是位於南大西洋的英國海外領土？

    A. Guernsey 根西島

    B. Northern Ireland 北愛爾蘭

    C. The Falkland Islands 福克蘭群島

    D. Jersey 澤西島

49. **Who wrote the novel 'Charlie and the Chocolate Factory'?**

    誰是《朱古力獎門人》小說的作者？

    A. Rudyard Kipling　拉迪亞德・吉卜林

    B. Sir William Golding　威廉・戈爾丁爵士

    C. Charles Dickens　查理・狄更斯

    D. Roald Dahl　朗奴・達爾

50. **The official name of the UK is:**

    英國的全名為：

    A. The United Kingdom of Great Britain and Southern Ireland
       大不列顛及南愛爾蘭聯合王國

    B. The Great Britain and Southern Ireland
       大不列顛和南愛爾蘭

    C. The United Kingdom of Great Britain and Northern Ireland
       大不列顛及北愛爾蘭聯合王國

    D. The United Kingdom and Great Ireland
       英國和大愛爾蘭

51. **What is the name of the first formal anti - slavery groups established in the late 1700s?**

    1700 年代後期成立首個正式的反奴隸組織，其名稱是什麼？

    A. Beefeaters　衛兵

    B. Suffragettes　參政者

    C. Quakers　貴格會

    D. Canutes　克努特

52. **When was slavery abolished throughout the British Empire?**

英國於哪一年廢除奴隸制度？

A. 1833

B 1843

C. 1844

D. 1861

53. **Magistrates and Justices of the Peace (JPs) are members of _____.**

裁判司和太平紳士是_____的成員？

A. Government　政府

B. Local community　當地社區

C. British Society　英國社會

D. National Health Society　國民保健署

54. **How can I find details about the small claims legal procedure?**

從哪裡可以獲得小額索賠法律程序的相關資訊？

A. From the local community　當地社區

B. At the police station　警局

C. At your local County Court or Sheriff Court　地方法院

D. At any local shop　任何商店

55. What is Mothering Sunday in the UK?

「英國母親日」是在：

A. The Sunday three weeks before Easter

復活節前三個禮拜的星期天

B. The Sunday three weeks after Easter

復活節後三個禮拜的星期日

C. The Sunday three weeks before Christmas

聖誕節前三個禮拜的星期天

D. The Sunday three weeks after Christmas

聖誕節後三個禮拜的星期天

56. When did modern tennis evolve in England?

現代網球在英國什麼時候發展起來？

A. early 18th century 十八世紀初

B. late 18th century 十八世紀後期

C. early 19th century 十九世紀初

D. late 19th century 十九世紀後期

57. When did the Crimean War start and end?

克里米亞戰爭從哪一年開始？又於哪一年結束？

A. 1850, 1853

B. 1851, 1854

C. 1852, 1855

D. 1853, 1856

58. **When did William of Orange claim the English throne?**

威廉‧奧蘭治於哪一年入侵英格蘭，並自稱為王？

A. 1689

B. 1690

C. 1688

D. 1687

59. **Which British painter below is considered to be the one who raised the importance of landscape painting?**

以下哪位英國畫家被認為是提升山水畫重要性的藝術家？

A. Joseph Turner　約瑟‧丹拿

B. David Allan　大衛‧亞倫

C. John Constable　約翰‧康斯特布爾

D. Sir John Lavery　約翰‧拉弗里爵士

60. **How long (in feet) is the Bayeux Tapestry?**

貝葉掛毯長幾多英呎？

A. 130

B. 230

C. 330

D. 320

61. **Which of the following countries is not a member of the Commonwealth?**

以下哪個國家不是英聯邦的成員國？

A. Swaziland　史瓦帝尼王國

B　Trinidad and Tobago　千里達及托巴哥共和國

C. Dominica　多明尼加

D. Costa Rica　哥斯達黎加

62. **Which of the following public services can be controlled by the devolved administrations?**

以下哪種公共服務由權力下放部門管理？

A. Defence　軍事防衛

B. Immigration　移民

C. Foreign Affairs　外交事務

D. Education　教育

63. **Which night is Bonfire Night ?**

焰火節（又叫篝火之夜）是什麼時候慶祝？

A. Sep 5　九月五日

B. Nov 5　十一月五日

C. Sep 15　九月十五日

D. Nov 15　十一月十五日

64. What was introduced by the 1944 Education Act?

1944 年的《教育法》為英國帶來了什麼？

A. Free primary education in England and Wales

為英格蘭和威爾斯，引入免費小學教育。

B. Free secondary education in England and Wales

為英格蘭和威爾斯，引入免費中學教育。

C. Free high school education in England and Wales

為英格蘭和威爾斯，引入免費高中教育。

D. Free university education in England and Wales

為英格蘭和威爾斯，引入免費大學教育。

65. What is the name of the event which refers to the 6 June 1944 when Allied Forces landed in Normandy aiming to attack Hitler's forces in Western Europe during World War II?

1944 年 6 月 6 日盟軍登陸諾曼第，目的是在第二次世界大戰期間攻擊希特拉西歐軍隊一事，又名為：

A. D - Day　D 日

B. Domesday　末日

C. A - Day　A 日

D. Allies Day　盟友日

66. Who led the Conservative government from 1979 to 1990?

誰在 1979 至 1990 年期間，領導保守黨政府？

A. John Major　馬卓安

B. Harold Macmillan　麥克米倫

C. Margaret Thatcher　戴卓爾夫人

D. Sir Alec Douglas - Home　亞歷克・道格拉斯 - 休姆爵士

67. Which of the following civilisations is known for having built roads and public buildings, creating a structure of law and having introduced new plants and animals in Britain?

哪個文明以修建道路和公共建築、建立法律結構，以及在英國引進新的動物和植物而聞名？

A. The Romans　羅馬人

B. The Vikings　維京人

C. The Normans　諾曼人

D. The Germans　德國人

68. How often is the Edinburgh Festival Fringe?

愛丁堡國際藝穗節多久舉行一次？

A. Every six months　每半年

B. Every summer　每年夏天

C. Every spring　每年春天

D. Every month　每個月

69. Which playwright had a great influence on the English language?

哪位英國劇作家對英語作出巨大貢獻？

A. William Shakespeare　威廉·莎士比亞

B. Graham Greene　格雷厄姆·格林

C. Dylan Thomas　狄蘭·湯瑪士

D. Harold Pinter　哈洛·品特

70. **In Britain, when is the birth of Jesus Christ celebrated?**

英國人每年會在什麼時候，慶祝耶穌基督誕生？

A. Dec 24　十二月廿四日

B. Dec 25　十二月廿五日

C. Dec 26　十二月廿六日

D. Dec 31　十二月卅一日

71. **Which political party did Margaret Thatcher belong to?**

戴卓爾夫人屬於哪個政黨？

A. Green Party　綠黨

B. Conservative Party　保守黨

C. Liberal Democrats Party　自由民主黨

D. Democratic Unionist Party　民主統一黨

72. **Which sport is played at Wimbledon?**

溫布頓錦標賽的比賽項目是什麼？

A. Football　足球

B. Tennis　網球

C. Rugby　欖球

D. Cricket　板球

73. **If you are found driving while exceeding the alcohol limit, you will:**

   假如被發現醉酒駕駛，你將會：

   A. not be allowed to drive again　被禁止再駕車

   B. be taken to the hospital　被送院

   C. be arrested　被捕

   D. be taken home by police　被警察送返住所

74. **Which of the following is a traditional pub game?**

   以下哪個是傳統酒吧遊戲？

   A. Darts　飛鏢

   B. Hide and seek　捉迷藏

   C. Bingo　賓果

   D. Checkers　跳棋

75. **Which of the following is NOT a fundamental principle of British life?**

   以下哪項不是英國生活的基本原則？

   A. Individual liberty　個人自由

   B. Democracy　民主

   C. Communism　共產主義

   D. Participation in community life　參與社區生活

2.1 Answers
答案及解題 (單選題：四選一)

1. C

Rugby originated in England in the early 19th century.

欖球起源於 19 世紀初的英國。

2. A

Between 1680 and 1720, many refugees called 'Huguenots' came from France. They were Protestants and had been persecuted for their religion.

很多法國難民於 1680 至 1720 年湧入英國，這些被稱為「胡格諾派」的人多為新教徒，他們因宗教信仰遭到迫害。

3. B

The Parliament of Northern Ireland was bicameral, consisting of a House of Commons with 52 seats, and an indirectly elected Senate with 26 seats.

北愛爾蘭議會實行「兩院制」，下議院有 52 個席位，至於由間接選舉產生的參議院則有 26 席。

4. C

Isaac Newton's most famous published work was Philosophiae Naturalis Principia Mathematica (Mathematical Principle of Natural Philosophy), which showed how gravity applied to the whole universe.

艾薩克•牛頓的著作《自然哲學的數學原理》，便展示了引力如何應用於整個宇宙。

5. A

George Frederick Handel wrote the Water Music for King George I and Music for the Royal Fireworks for his son, George II.

喬治•弗雷德里克•亨德爾首先為喬治一世國王創作了水上音樂，後來又為後者的兒子喬治二世，創作皇家煙花音樂。

6. C

The Civil War between the King and Parliament began in 1642.

英國內戰是指由 1642 至 1651 年發生於「議會派」與「保皇派」之間的武裝衝突及政治鬥爭。

7. D

The London Eye was originally built as part of the UK's celebration of the new millennium and continues to be an important part of New Year celebrations.

「倫敦眼」原本是為英國慶祝新千年的一部分而建造，現在仍然用作慶祝新年的活動地點。

8. C

Parliamentary democracy means that U.K. nationals have the power to elect their legislative representatives, whose work is to present the citizen's interests to the government.

議會民主是指英國國民有權選舉他們的立法代表，他們的工作是向政府展示國民的利益。

9. D

The Spanish Armada was a large fleet of ships, which had been sent by Spain to conquer England and restore Catholicism.

「西班牙無敵艦隊」是一支龐大的船隊，由西班牙調派往征服英格蘭，以圖恢復天主教的地位。

10. A

In 1314 the Scottish, led by Robert the Bruce, defeated the English at the Battle of Bannockburn.

1314 年，由羅拔·布魯士率領的蘇格蘭軍隊，於班諾克本戰役中擊敗英軍。

11. C

Prince Philip was 99 years old when he died. He was born on June 10, 1921.

菲臘親王去世時享年 99 歲，他生於 1921 年 6 月 10 日。

12. D

The Millennium Stadium is located in Cardiff (the capital of Wales). It is also known as Principality Stadium.

千禧球場位於威爾斯首都卡迪夫,該球場又被稱為「威爾斯國家體育場」。

13. C

The Clans lost a lot of their power after the Battle of Culloden in 1746.

卡洛登戰役在 1746 年結束後,氏族大大地失去了權力和影響力。

14. A

Wastwater is also England's deepest lake: 258 feet (about 79 m).

沃斯特湖同時也是英格蘭最深的湖泊:水深達 258 英呎(約 79 米)。

15. C

From 1695, newspapers were allowed to operate without a government license. Increasing numbers of newspapers began to be published.

從 1695 年起,由於報章可以在沒有政府發牌的情況下經營,令越來越多報紙出現。

16. C

The Norman Conquest was the last successful foreign invasion of England and led to many changes in government and social structures in England.

「諾曼征服」是英格蘭最後一次成功侵佔別國的戰爭,戰事更導致英格蘭政府和社會結構出現多重變化。

17. D

Richard Austen Butler became a Conservative MP in 1923 and held several positions before becoming responsible for education in 1941. He was generally known as R. A. Butler and familiarly known from his initials as 'Rab'.

李察•奧斯丁•畢拿於 1923 年成為保守黨國會議員,並在 1941 年負責教育事務之前,出任過多個職位。有時為方便起見,人們會用其名字 Richard Austen Butler 的姓名首字母「Rab」來代表他。

18. A

Isaac Newton was born in Lincolnshire, eastern England.

艾薩克•牛頓出生於英格蘭東部的林肯郡。

19. B

The Kingdom of Great Britain was created under The Act of Union 1707.

大不列顛王國是根據《1707 年聯合法令》創建。

20. A

There is a National Horseracing Museum in Newmarket, Suffolk.

賽馬博物館設於沙福郡新市。

21. C

Croatia became a member state in 2013.

克羅地亞在 2013 年加入歐盟。

22. D

The first Women's Social and Political Union Group (founded in 1903) members were called Suffragettes.

1903 年成立的「婦女社會和政治聯盟」，其成員叫婦女參政運動者。

23. A

In Boer War, the British went to war in South Africa with settlers from the Netherlands called the Boers.

在布爾戰爭中，英軍在南非與來自荷蘭的布爾人開戰。

24. B

The Battle of Agincourt broke out on Oct 25, 1415.

阿金庫爾戰役（或稱愛靜閣戰役）於 1415 年10 月 25 日爆發。

25. D

The development of the Bessemer steel making process for the mass production of steel led to the development of the shipbuilding industry and the railways.

大規模生產鋼鐵的「貝塞麥鍊鋼法」帶動造船業和鐵路業發展。

26. D

England won the World Cup in 1966 when it was captained by Bobby Moore.

英格蘭國家足球隊在 1966 年贏得世界盃，球隊當時由卜比•摩亞擔任隊長。

27. B

Britain's navy fought against combined French and Spanish fleets, winning the Battle of Trafalgar in 1805.

英國海軍與法國和西班牙的聯合艦隊對戰，最後贏得了 1805 年的特拉法加海戰。

28. C

In the middle of the 19th century the potato crop failed, and Ireland suffered a famine. A million people died from disease and starvation.

在 19 世紀中葉，愛爾蘭因馬鈴薯等農作物失收，令舉國上下遭受饑荒。據悉，因疾病和飢餓而死的人數多達 100 萬。

29. C

Hitler wanted to invade Britain, but before sending in troops, Germany needed to control the air campaign against Britain, but the British resisted with their fighter planes and eventually won the crucial aerial battle against the Germans, called 'the Battle of Britain'.

當時德國的希特拉想入侵英國，但它需要控制對英國的空中勢力範圍。不過，英軍最後利用戰鬥機反抗，並成功擊退德軍，史稱「不列顛戰役」（又名英倫空戰）。

30. B

PCCs (Police and Crime Commissioners) set local police priorities and the local policing budget. They also appoint the local Chief Constable.

PCCs（警察和犯罪專員）除制定本地警察的工作事項和財務預算外，更要負責任命當地警察局長的工作。

31. A

The British attack of the Somme in July 1916, resulted in about 60,000 British casualties on the first day alone.

英國於 1916 年 7 月攻打索姆河，然而僅在戰事第一天，就錄得約 6 萬名英國人傷亡。

32. D

The first Union Flag was created in 1606 from the flags of Scotland and England, the Principality of Wales was already united with England. Besides, 'Union Flag' is also called the Union Jack, British flag or UK flag.

1606 年，第一面聯合國旗由蘇格蘭和英格蘭的國旗創建，當時威爾斯經已與英格蘭結盟。此外，聯合旗有其他別稱，例如米字旗、聯合積克。

33. B

'Big Ben' is the nickname for the great bell of the clock at the Houses of Parliament in London.

大本鐘是倫敦國會大廈大鐘的暱稱。

34. B

Anne Boleyn was executed at the tower of London.

安妮•博林在倫敦塔被處決。

35. A

Britain has produced many great designers, from Thomas Chippendale (who designed furniture in the 18th century) to Clarice Cliff (who designed Art Deco ceramics) to Sir Terence Conran (a 20th century interior designer).

英國培育了許多偉大的設計師，從 Thomas Chippendale（18 世紀設計家具）到 Clarice Cliff（設計裝飾藝術陶瓷），再到 Terence Conran 爵士（20 世紀室內設計師）。

36. C

Bradford is located in England.

巴拉福特位於英格蘭。

37. B

In 1066, an invasion led by William, the Duke of Normandy, defeated Harold, the Saxon king of England, at the Battle of Hastings. Harold was killed in the battle.

在 1066 年，諾曼第公爵威廉在「黑斯廷斯戰役」中，擊敗英格蘭撒克遜國王哈羅德，後者在戰鬥中陣亡。

38. B

Court orders can be obtained to protect a person from being forced into a marriage, or to protect a person in a forced marriage.

個人可以獲得法院命令，保障其免被強迫結婚。

39. C

The BBC started radio broadcasts in 1922 and began the world's first regular television service in 1936.

英國廣播公司於 1922 年開始無線電廣播，並於 1936 年開始進行世界上首個常規電視服務。

40. C

During WWII as France fell, the British decided to evacuate British and French soldiers from France in a huge naval operation. Many civilian volunteers in small pleasure and fishing boats from Britain helped the Navy to rescue more than 300,000 men from the beaches around Dunkirk. The evacuation gave rise to the phrase 'the Dunkirk spirit'.

隨著法國在第二次世界大戰期間淪陷，英國決定在一次大規模的海軍行動中，從法國撤離英、法士兵。許多來自英國的遊樂船和漁船的平民志願者，幫助海軍從鄧寇克附近的海灘，營救了超過 30 萬名士兵，該次大規模撤離行動，衍生了「鄧寇克精神」的名詞。

41. C

The National Citizen Service (NCS) programme gives 16- and 17-year-olds the opportunity to enjoy outdoor activities, develop their skills and take part in a community project.

全國公民服務（NCS）計劃讓 16 至 17 歲的青少年有機會享受戶外活動、發展他們的技能，並參與社區項目。

However, you can go on programme as a 15-year-old, as long as you turn 16 on or by 31 August of the year you apply for. If you have already turned 18 by this date, you unfortunately won't be eligible.

不過，只要你在申請當年的 8 月 31 日前年滿 16 歲，你便可以在 15 歲時繼續該計劃。但如果你在此日期之前已年滿 18 歲，那你便不合資格。

42. A

In 1837, Queen Victoria became queen of the UK at the age of 18.

維多利亞女王於 1837 年成為女王，當時她只有 18 歲。

43. D

Jane Austen was an English novelist. Her books include Pride and Prejudice and Sense and Sensibility.

珍‧奧斯丁是英國一名女作家，其著作包括《傲慢與偏見》和《理智與情感》。

44. B

Women could vote at 21, the same age as men.

凡年滿 21 歲的女性都擁有投票權，與男性地位相等。

45. B

The Scottish architect Robert Adam designed the inside decoration as well as the building itself in great houses such as Dumfries House in Scotland.

鄧弗里斯莊園是由蘇格蘭著名建築師羅拔・亞當親自設計。

46. D

Britain was invaded by tribes from northern Europe: the Jutes, the Angles and the Saxons in the past.

英國曾先後被來自北歐的部落入侵，這些部落包括：朱特人、盎格魯人和撒克遜人。

47. B

The most famous sailing event in the UK takes place at Cowes on the Isle of Wight.

英國最著名的帆船賽事在懷特島的考斯舉行。

48. C

The Falkland Islands, a British overseas territory is located in the South Atlantic.

位於南大西洋的福克蘭群島，屬於英國的海外領土。

49. D

Roald Dahl is the author of Charlie and the Chocolate Factory.

朗奴・達爾是《朱古力獎門人》小說的作者。

50. C

The official name of the country is the United Kingdom of Great Britain and Northern Ireland.

英國的全名為「大不列顛及北愛爾蘭聯合王國」。

51. C

The first formal anti-slavery groups were set up by the Quakers in the late 1700s, and they petitioned Parliament to ban the practice.

貴格會在 1700 年代後期成立第一個正式的反奴隸制組織，該組織要求議會禁止奴隸活動。

52. A

In 1833, the Emancipation Act abolished slavery throughout the British Empire.

1833 年，《解放法案》廢除了整個大英帝國的奴隸制度。

53. B

Magistrates and Justices of the Peace (JPs) are members of the local community.

裁判司和太平紳士是當地社區的成員。

54. C

You can get details about the small claims procedure from your local County Court or Sheriff Court.

你可以從地方法院獲得有關小額索賠程序的詳細信息。

55. A

Mothering Sunday (or Mother's day) is the Sunday three weeks before Easter. Children send cards or buy gifts for their mothers.

英國母親日（或母親節）是復活節前三星期的星期日，孩子們會為媽媽送上心意咭或買禮物。

56. D

Modern tennis evolved in England in the late 19th century.

現代網球在 19 世紀後期，於英格蘭發展起來。

57. D

From 1853 to 1856, Britain fought with Turkey and France against Russia in the Crimean War.

從 1853 至 1856 年，英國在克里米亞戰爭中與土耳其和法國共同對抗俄羅斯，最終俄羅斯敗陣。

58. C

In 1688, important Protestants in England asked William of Orange to invade England and proclaim himself king. When William reached England, there was no resistance. James fled to France and William took over the throne, becoming William III in England, Wales and Ireland, and William II of Scotland.

1688 年，英格蘭重要的新教徒要求威廉·奧蘭治入侵英格蘭，並宣稱自己為國王。當威廉到達英國時，並未有遭遇到抵抗。占士逃到法國，威廉繼位，後者成為英格蘭、威爾斯和愛爾蘭的威廉三世和蘇格蘭的威廉二世。

59. A

Joseph Turner was an influential landscape painter in a modern style. He is considered the artist who raised the profile of landscape painting.

約瑟·丹拿是一位具有影響力的現代風格的風景畫家，他被外界認為是提升山水畫形象的英國藝術家。

60. B

Bayeux Tapestry, the National Treasure of France in the 11th Century, is nearly 70 meters (about 230 feet) long and is embroidered with coloured wool.

法國 11 世紀國寶「貝葉掛毯」長近 70 米（約 230 英呎），上面繡有彩色羊毛。

61. D

Costa Rica is not a member of the Commonwealth.

哥斯達黎加並不屬於英聯邦成員國。

62. D

Some public services, such as education, are controlled by the devolved administrations.

一些公共服務（如教育），由權力下放的行政部門控制。

63. B

Bonfire Night is celebrated on Nov 5.

11 月 5 日慶祝焰火節。

64. B

The 1944 Education Act (often called 'The Butler Act'), introduced free secondary education in England and Wales.

1944 年通過的「教育法」（又稱巴特勒法案），為英格蘭和威爾斯引入免費中學教育。

65. A

'D-Day' refers to the 6th of June 1944, when allied forces landed in Normandy aiming to attack Hitler's forces in Western Europe during World War II.

「諾曼第登陸日」指 1944 年 6 月 6 日，當時盟軍登陸諾曼第，目標是在第二次世界大戰期間，攻擊希特拉在西歐的軍隊。

66. C

Margaret Thatcher, Britain's first woman Prime Minister, led the Conservative government from 1979 to 1990.

戴卓爾夫人為英國第一位女性擔任首相的人，她於 1979 至 1990 年領導保守黨政府。

67. A

The Romans remained in Britain around 400 years. They built roads and public buildings, created a structure of law, and introduced new plants and animals.

羅馬人統治英國約 400 年。他們修建道路和公共建築，又建立了法律結構，並引進了新的動物和植物。

68. B

The Edinburgh Festival Fringe takes place in Edinburgh, Scotland, every summer.

愛丁堡國際藝穗節每年夏天在蘇格蘭愛丁堡舉行。

69. A

Shakespeare had a great influence on the English language and invented many words that are still common today.

莎士比亞對英語產生重大的影響，許多我們時下常用的字詞，都是由其所創。

70. B

In Britain, the birth of Jesus Christ will be celebrated on Dec 25.

英國每年會在 12 月 25 日慶祝耶穌基督誕生。

71. B

Margaret Thatcher led the Conservative government from 1979 to 1990.

戴卓爾夫人是英國保守黨的一員，並於 1979 至 1990 年領導保守黨政府。

72. B

The most famous tennis tournament hosted in Britain is The Wimbledon Championships, which takes place each year at the All England Lawn Tennis and Croquet Club.

在英國舉辦的最著名的網球錦標賽是溫布頓錦標賽，每年都會在「全英草地網球和槌球俱樂部」舉行。

73. C

If you are found driving while exceeding the alcohol limit, you will be arrested.

假如被發現醉酒駕駛，你將會被捕。

74. A

Pool and darts are traditional pub games.

桌球和飛鏢都是英國傳統酒吧遊戲。

75. C

The five British Values are: democracy, the rule of law, individual liberty, mutual respect, tolerance of those of different faiths and beliefs.

英國生活的基本原則包括：民主、法治、個人自由、包容不同信仰，以及參與社區生活。

2.2 正誤判斷題

Decide whether a statement Is true or false.
確定陳述是對還是錯。

1. **The Romans ruled Britain for 500 years.**
   羅馬人統治了英國 500 年。
   A. True　正確
   B. False　錯誤

2. **To vote in elections, you must register at your local council's Electoral Registration Office.**
   如要投票，你必須到地區議會選舉登記處辦登記手續。
   A. True　正確
   B. False　錯誤

3. **It is an offense not to have an MOT (Ministry of Transport) certificate if your vehicle is more than two years old or without car insurance.**
   如果閣下的座駕未附有由英國交通部簽發的合格證，而車齡超過兩年，或未有購買汽車保險，便屬違法。
   A. True　正確
   B. False　錯誤

4. **Sir Robert Watson Watt proposed that enemy aircrafts could be detected by radio waves.**

    羅拔・華生・瓦特提出通過無線電波探測敵機。

    A. True　正確

    B. False　錯誤

5. **Robert Louis Stevenson, Graham Greene and Sir Kingsley Amis were British writers.**

    羅拔史蒂文森、格雷厄姆格林，以及金斯利艾米斯爵士，以上三人都是英國作家。

    A. True　正確

    B. False　錯誤

6. **Since 2007, there have been more female students in higher education than male.**

    自 2007 年起，接受高等教育的在學女性，數目比男性要多。

    A. True　正確

    B. False　錯誤

7. **People on the electoral register whose age between 18 and 65 can be asked to serve on a jury.**

    在選民登記冊上，年齡界乎 18 至 65 歲的人，都有機會獲邀做陪審團。

    A. True　正確

    B. False　錯誤

8. **Women in Britain today occupy about 40% of the workforce.**

今日的英國女性，佔整體勞動力約四成。

A. True　正確

B. False　錯誤

9. **Many schools organize events like selling books, toys or food in order to raise money for extra equipment or out-of-school activities.**

許多學校組織活動如售賣書籍、玩具或食物，以籌集額外設備或用作舉辦課外活動的資金。

A. True　正確

B. False　錯誤

10. **It is free to watch television on mobile devices.**

你可以透過流動電話免費收看電視節目。

A. True　正確

B. False　錯誤

11. **The female employment rate was 62% in October to December 2021.**

英國女性在 2021 年 10 至 12 月的就業率為 62%。

A. True　正確

B. False　錯誤

12. **On average, boys leave school with better qualifications than girls.**

男孩畢業時的學術成績平均比女孩高。

A. True　正確

B. False　錯誤

13. **The Northern Ireland Assembly has been suspended several times.**

北愛爾蘭地方議會曾多次遭暫停運作。

A. True　正確

B. False　錯誤

14. **The Reform Act of 1832 increased the amount of people who had the right to vote.**

1832 年《改革法案》的通過，令投票人數得以擴大。

A. True　正確

B. False　錯誤

15. **If a man forces his wife to have sex with him, he can be arrested and charged with rape.**

假如一名丈夫強迫妻子發生性關係，他將有機會被控以強姦罪。

A. True　正確

B. False　錯誤

16. Pet owners are responsible for keeping their dog under control, and also for cleaning up after your dog in public places to keep the environment clean.

狗主有責任清理犬隻在公眾場合便溺後的污垢。

A. True　正確

B. False　錯誤

17. In England and Wales, it is illegal to crop a dog's ears.

在英格蘭和威爾斯，剪掉狗隻的耳朵是違法的。

A. True　正確

B. False　錯誤

18. Life in the UK test is usually taken in English. Special arrangements can be made if one wishes to take it in another language like French.

英國永居及入籍試一般以英語進行，考生如欲以其他語言（如法語）應考，有關方面可作出特別安排。

A. True　正確

B. False　錯誤

19. The right to a fair trial is not included amongst the principles of the European Convention of Human Rights.

獲得公平審判的權利，並不寫在《歐洲人權公約》的原則中。

A. True　正確

B. False　錯誤

20. Elizabeth I never married and so had no children of her own to inherit her throne.

伊莉莎白一世因未婚，故沒有子女繼承王位。

A. True　正確

B. False　錯誤

21. UK laws ensure that people are not treated unfairly in any area of life or work because of their age, disability, sex, pregnancy and maternity, race, religion or belief, sexuality or marital status.

英國法律確保人們不會因年齡、殘疾、性別、懷孕和生育、種族、宗教或信仰、性取向或婚姻狀況，而在生活或工作的任何領域上，受到不公平的對待。

A. True　正確

B. False　錯誤

22. England more or less consistently makes up 70% of the total population of the UK.

英格蘭約佔英國總人口的 7 成。

A. True　正確

B. False　錯誤

23. At the beginning of the Middle Ages, Ireland was an independent country.

早在中世紀初，愛爾蘭經已是一個獨立國家。

A. True　正確

B. False　錯誤

24. Since 1997, some powers have been devolved from the central government to give people living in Wales, Scotland and Northern Ireland more control over matters that directly affect them.

自 1997 年起，中央政府下放部分權力，賦予威爾斯、蘇格蘭和北愛爾蘭人民，對直接影響他們的事務有更多控制權。

A. True　正確

B. False　錯誤

25. As part of the citizenship ceremony, new British citizens pledge their loyalty to the United Kingdom and to respect its rights and freedoms.

作為入籍英國儀式的一部分，新公民須宣誓效忠聯合王國，並尊重其權利和自由。

A. True　正確

B. False　錯誤

26. Every person in the UK receives equal treatment under the law. This means that the law applies in the same way to everyone, no matter who they are or where they are from.

在英國，每個人都受到平等法律待遇，意味著法律以同樣的方式適用於所有人，不管他們是誰或來自哪裡。

A. True　正確

B. False　錯誤

27. **After Oliver Cromwell defeated the Scottish army in the Battles of Dunbar and Worcester, Charles II escaped from Worcester, famously hiding in an oak tree on one occasion, and eventually fled to Europe.**

奧利華・克倫威爾在鄧巴和伍斯特戰役擊敗蘇格蘭軍隊後，查理二世逃離伍斯特郡，後者並因一次躲在橡樹中的事件聞名。查理二世最終逃往歐洲。

A. True　正確

B. False　錯誤

28. **By 1200, the English ruled an area of Scotland around Edinburgh, which is known as 'The Pale'.**

到 1200 年，英國人在愛丁堡附近統治了蘇格蘭的帕萊地區。

A. True　正確

B. False　錯誤

29. **NSPCC refers to 'the National Society for Promoting Community Communication'. It helps immigrants integrate into the community.**

NSPCC 的全名為 the National Society for the Promoting Community Communication（全國促進社區交流協會），協會的主要工作是幫助外來移民加速融入社區。

A. True　正確

B. False　錯誤

30. **After the Second World War, the UK was economically exhausted.**

英國經濟在第二次世界大戰後變得疲憊。

A. True　正確

B. False　錯誤

31. **Bonfire Night remembers the day which a group of Catholics led by Guy Fawkes. Members successfully killed the Protestant king with a bomb in the Houses of Parliament.**

英國焰火節（或稱篝火之夜）令人回憶起由蓋伊・福克斯領導的天主教徒，於國會大廈成功炸死新教國王一事。

A. True　正確

B. False　錯誤

32. **Arranged marriages are not acceptable in the UK.**

英國並不接受「包辦婚姻」。

A. True　正確

B. False　錯誤

33. **Queen Elizabeth I was a Catholic.**

伊莉莎白一世是天主教徒。

A. True　正確

B. False　錯誤

34. **Charles I wanted the worship of the Church of England to include more ceremony. He later introduced a revised Prayer Book.**

查理一世希望令英格蘭教會的崇拜儀式變得更豐富，他後來對祈禱書作出增訂。

A. True　正確

B. False　錯誤

35. **The Magna Carta protected the rights of the nobility and restricted the king's power to collect taxes or to make or change laws.**

大憲章保障了貴族的利益，並限制君主收稅、制訂或修改法律的權力。

A. True　正確

B. False　錯誤

36. **Walter Scott wrote poems inspired by Scotland and the traditional stories and songs from the area on the borders of Scotland and England.**

華特・史葛的詩歌，靈感來自蘇格蘭以及蘇格蘭和英格蘭邊界地區的傳統故事和歌曲。

A. True　正確

B. False　錯誤

37. **The bell called Big Ben, housed in the Elizabeth Tower, is over 200 years old and is a popular tourist attraction.**

位於伊莉莎白塔、名為「大本鐘」的旅遊景點，擁有超過 200 年的歷史。

A. True　正確

B. False　錯誤

38. **St Patrick's day is a public holiday in Northern Ireland**

聖帕特里克節是北愛爾蘭的公共假日。

A. True　正確

B. False　錯誤

39. **British values and principles are based on history and traditions and are protected by law, customs and expectations.**

英國的價值觀和原則是以歷史和傳統為基礎，並受到法律、習俗和期望的保障。

A. True　正確

B. False　錯誤

40. **St. Peter is the patron saint of Wales and on 29th November is his feast day.**

聖彼德是威爾斯的守護神，他的節日是 11 月 29 日。

A. True　正確

B. False　錯誤

41. **The Laurence Olivier Awards take place annually at London Film Academy in London. There are a variety of categories, including best director, best actor and best actress.**

「羅蘭士・奧利花劇場頒獎禮」每年都會於倫敦電影學院舉行。該典禮設多個類別的獎項，包括最佳導演獎、最佳男演員獎，以及最佳女演員獎。

A. True　正確

B. False　錯誤

42. **The Laurence Olivier Awards are named after the British actor Sir Laurence Olivier, later Lord Olivier, who was best known for his roles in various Charles Dickens plays.**

「羅蘭士・奧利花劇場頒獎禮」以英國演員勞倫斯・奧利維爾爵士（即後來的奧利維爾勳爵）的名字命名，他以在查理・狄更斯中的劇作而聞名。

A. True　正確

B. False　錯誤

43. **Henry VIII took the English throne after the death of Edward VI.**

愛德華六世死後，王位由亨利八世繼承。

A. True　正確

B. False　錯誤

44. **Catherine Parr gave Henry VIII the son he wanted, Edward.**
凱瑟琳・帕爾給了亨利八世他想要的兒子：愛德華。
A. True　正確
B. False　錯誤

45. **Carrying a weapon is a criminal offense, unless it is for the reason of self-defense.**
攜帶武器屬刑事罪行，除非行為是基於自衛。
A. True　正確
B. False　錯誤

46. **The Harrier jump jet, an aircraft capable of taking off vertically, was imported from the United States.**
獵鷹式戰鬥機是一種能夠垂直起飛的飛機，是從美國進口。
A. True　正確
B. False　錯誤

47. **You can get a job and start to work even without a National Insurance number.**
即使未獲發國民保險號碼，你仍可在英國找到工作。
A. True　正確
B. False　錯誤

48. **The Speaker of the House of Commons, is a neutral MP (members of Parliament) and does not represent a political party.**

下議院議長的地位中立，並不代表某個政黨。

A. True　正確

B. False　錯誤

49. **When Cromwell died, his son Richard, became the Lord Protector in his place. However, Richard was not able to control the army or the government.**

克倫威爾死後，兒子李察接替他成為護國公，但即使如此，卻仍然無法控制軍隊或政府。

A. True　正確

B. False　錯誤

50. **Elections helds in Britain every 4 years.**

英國每隔四年會舉行一次選舉。

A. True　正確

B. False　錯誤

51. **The UK is part of the United Nations.**

英國是聯合國的一部分。

A. True　正確

B. False　錯誤

52. **Sir Francis Drake, one of the commanders in the defeat of the American Armada.**

弗朗西斯・德雷克爵士是擊敗「美國無敵艦隊」的指揮官之一。

A. True　正確

B. False　錯誤

53. **The ship 'Golden Hind' is related to Hindu.**

船隻 Golden Hind 跟印度教有關。

A. True　正確

B. False　錯誤

54. **The Union Flag has four crosses.**

英國國旗（或稱聯合旗）上有四個交叉十字圖案。

A. True　正確

B. False　錯誤

55. **The devolved administrations of Wales, Scotland and Northern Ireland each have their own civil service.**

威爾斯、蘇格蘭和北愛爾蘭的權力下放政府，各有自己的公務員。

A. True　正確

B. False　錯誤

56. 'National Lottery' draws every wednesday and sundays.

英國每逢星期三、日，都會進行國家彩票攪珠。

A. True 　正確

B. False 　錯誤

57. Anyone who is violent towards their partner – whether they are a man or a woman, married or living together – can be prosecuted.

任何對伴侶暴力的人——無論是男人還是女人，已婚還是同居——都可以被起訴。

A. True 　正確

B. False 　錯誤

58. The Queen's Open is the name of the only 'Grand Slam' tennis event played on grass.

女王公開賽是唯一於草地上進行的「大滿貫」網球賽事名稱。

A. True 　正確

B. False 　錯誤

59. The term 'Habeas corpus' means you must present the person in court.

「人身保護令」是指你必須在法庭上出示任何人。

A. True 　正確

B. False 　錯誤

60. Ramadan is the name given to the candelabrum lit during Hanukkah.

光明節所點燃蠟燭的燭台叫 Ramadan。

A. True　正確

B. False　錯誤

61. 'The Enlightenment' is known as new ideas about politics, philosophy and science that were developed in the 17th century.

「啟蒙運動」是指在 17 世紀發展起來的關於政治、哲學和科學之新思想。

A. True　正確

B. False　錯誤

62. Queen Elizabeth II borned on 20th April, 1926.

伊莉莎白二世生於 1926 年 4 月 20 日。

A. True　正確

B. False　錯誤

63. During Halloween people carve lanterns out of Pumpkins and put a candle inside of them.

在萬聖節期間，人們會用南瓜雕刻燈籠，並在裡面放一支蠟燭。

A. True　正確

B. False　錯誤

64. **Ireland became unified with England, Wales and Scotland in 1800.**

愛爾蘭於 1800 年與英格蘭、威爾斯和蘇格蘭統一。

A. True　正確

B. False　錯誤

65. **Henry Purcell was an opera composer.**

亨利・珀塞爾是歌劇作曲家。

A. True　正確

B. False　錯誤

66. **Life peers are appointed by the Prime Minister on the advice of the Queen.**

終身貴族是由首相根據女王的建議任命。

A. True　正確

B. False　錯誤

67. **The Giant's Causeway is located in the South-west coast of England.**

巨人堤道位於英格蘭的西南海岸。

A. True　正確

B. False　錯誤

2.2 Answers
答案及解題（正誤判斷題）

1. B - False 錯誤

The Romans ruled Britain for about 400 years (from 43 A.D. to 410 A.D.)

羅馬統治英國約 400 年（由公元 43 至 410 年）。

2. A - True 正確

To vote in elections, you must register at your local council's Electoral Registration Office.

如要投票，你必須到地區議會選舉登記處辦登記手續。

3. B - False 錯誤

It is an offense not to have an MOT certificate if your vehicle is more than THREE years old or without car insurance.

如果閣下的座駕未附有由英國交通部簽發的合格證，而車齡超過 3 年，或未有購買汽車保險，便屬違法。

4. A - True 正確

The radar was developed by Scotsman Sir Robert Watson-Watt, who proposed that enemy aircraft could be detected by radio waves. The first successful radar test took place in 1935.

雷達是由蘇格蘭人羅拔・華生・瓦特爵士開發，他提出可以通過無線電波探測到敵機。第一次成功的雷達測試發生在 1935 年。

5. A - True 正確

a. Robert Louis Stevenson's literary work: Treasure Island, New Arabian Nights
羅拔・路易斯・史蒂文森著有《金銀島》、《新天方夜譚》
b. Graham Greene's literary work: The Heart of the Matter, The End of the Affair 格雷厄姆・格林著有《問題的核心》、《戀情的終結》
c. Sir Kingsley Amis's literary work: Lucky Jim 金斯利・艾米斯著有《幸運兒吉姆》

6. A - True 正確

Since 2007, the number of women in higher education has increased rapidly, and there are now nearly 67,000 more women enrolled in UK institutions than men.

自 2007 年以來，接受高等教育的女性人數迅速增加，目前在英國高等院校就讀的女性人數比男性多出接近 67,000 人。

7. B - False 錯誤

People on the electoral register will be randomly selected to serve on a jury. Anyone who is on the electoral register and age between 18 to 70 can be asked to do this.

凡已於選民登記冊上的人，只要年齡界乎 18 至 70 歲，都有機會被選中做陪審團。

8. B - False 錯誤

Women in Britain today make up about HALF of the workforce.

今天英國的女性約佔勞動力的一半。

9. A - True 正確

Many schools organize events like selling books, toys or food in order to raise money for extra equipment or out-of-school activities.

許多學校組織活動如售賣書籍、玩具或食物，以籌集額外設備或用作舉辦課外活動的資金。

10. B - False 錯誤

Everyone in the UK with a TV, computer or other medium which can be used for watching TV must have a 'television license': one license covers all of the equipment in one home, except when people rent different rooms in a shared house and each has a separate tenancy agreement — those people must each buy a separate license.

在英國，擁有電視、電腦或其他可用於觀看電視的媒體的每個人，都必須持有電視執照：一個許可證涵蓋一個家庭中的所有設備，除非人們在共享房屋中租用不同的房間，且每個人都有單獨的租賃協議——這些人必須各自購買單獨的許可證。

11. B - False 錯誤

According to the report 'Women and the UK economy 2022' revealed (published by the House of Commons), the female employment rate was 72.2% in October to December 2021, compared with 78.8% male employment rate.

根據英國下議院發表的報告「2022 年女性與英國經濟」指出,英國女性在 2021 年 10 至 12 月的就業率為 72.2%,至於男性就業率則為 78.8%。

12. B - False 錯誤

On average, girls leave school with better qualifications than boys.

平均而言,女孩在離開校園時,成績一般高於男孩。

13. A - True 正確

Since then the Assembly has operated with several interruptions and has been suspended on 5 occasions.

北愛爾蘭地方議會曾暫停運作過 5 次。

14. A - True 正確

The Reform Act 1832 introduced major changes to the electoral system of England and Wales. It abolished tiny districts, gave representation to cities, gave the vote to small landowners, tenant farmers, shopkeepers, householders who paid a yearly rental of £10 or more, and some lodgers.

《1832 年改革法案》對英格蘭和威爾斯的選舉制度,作出重大改革:法案廢除了小區,賦予城市代表權,將投票權授予小地主、佃農、店主、每年租金 10 英鎊或以上的業主以及一些租客。

15. A - True 正確

Any man who forces a woman to have sex, including a woman's husband, can be charged with rape.

任何強迫女性發生性行為的男性,即使施襲者與受害人份屬夫婦,前者都有機會被控以強姦罪。

16. A - True 正確

Pet owners are responsible for keeping their dog under control, and also for cleaning up after your dog in public places to keep the environment clean.

狗主有責任清理犬隻在公眾場合便溺後的污垢。

17. A - True 正確

It is illegal in England and Wales to crop a dog's ears, in whole or even in part. If you break the law, the penalties include a maximum of 6 months in prison and/or an unlimited fine.

在英格蘭和威爾斯，剪掉狗隻的耳朵（全部或部分）都是違法的。假如觸犯法例，處罰包括最多監禁 6 個月和 / 或無限罰款。

18. B - False 錯誤

Special arrangements can be made if you wish to take it in Welsh or Scottish Gaelic.

該些「特別安排」只限以威爾斯語，又或者用蘇格蘭蓋爾語應考的考生。

19. B - False 錯誤

The right to a fair trial is one of the principles of the European Convention of Human Rights.

獲得公平審判的權利是《歐洲人權公約》的一項原則。

20. A - True 正確

伊莉莎白一世因未未婚，故沒有子女繼承王位。

21. A - True 正確

UK laws ensure that people are not treated unfairly in any area of life or work because of their age, disability, sex, pregnancy and maternity, race, religion or belief, sexuality or marital status.

英國法律保障人們不會因年齡、殘疾、性別、懷孕和生育、種族、宗教或信仰、性取向或婚姻狀況，而在生活或工作的任何領域上，受到不公平的對待。

22. B - False 錯誤

The population is unequally distributed over the four parts of the UK: England more or less consistently makes up 84% of the total population,

Wales around 5%,

Scotland just over 8%, and

Northern Ireland less than 3%.

英國 4 個地區的人口分佈並不平均：英格蘭大約佔總人口的 84%，威爾斯約佔 5%，蘇格蘭略高於 8%，至於北愛爾蘭則少於 3%。

23. A - True 正確

At the beginning of the Middle Ages, Ireland was an independent country.

早在中世紀初，愛爾蘭經已是一個獨立國家。

24. A - True 正確

Since 1997, some powers have been devolved from the central government to give people living in Wales, Scotland and Northern Ireland more control over matters that directly affect them.

自 1997 年起，中央政府下放部分權力，賦予威爾斯、蘇格蘭和北愛爾蘭人民，對直接影響他們的事務有更多控制權。

25. A - True 正確

As part of the citizenship ceremony, new British citizens pledge their loyalty to the United Kingdom and to respect its rights and freedoms.

作為入籍英國儀式的一部分，新公民須宣誓效忠聯合王國，並尊重其權利和自由。

26. A - True 正確

Every person in the UK receives equal treatment under the law. This means that the law applies in the same way to everyone, no matter who they are or where they are from.

在英國，每個人都受到平等法律待遇，意味著法律以同樣的方式適用於所有人，不管他們是誰或來自哪裡。

27. A - True 正確

After Oliver Cromwell defeated the Scottish army in the Battles of Dunbar and Worcester, Charles II escaped from Worcester, famously hiding in an oak tree on one occasion, and eventually fled to Europe.

奧利華・克倫威爾在鄧巴和伍斯特戰役擊敗蘇格蘭軍隊後，查理二世逃離伍斯特郡，後者並因一次躲在橡樹中的事件聞名。查理二世最終逃往歐洲。

28. B - False 錯誤

By 1200, the English ruled an area of Ireland known as 'The Pale', near Dublin.

在 1200 年，英國人統治了愛爾蘭都柏林附近的帕萊地區。

29. B - False 錯誤

NSPCC refers to 'the National Society for the Prevention of Cruelty to Children', which is a British child protection charity.

NSPCC 的全名為 the National Society for the Prevention of Cruelty to Children （全國防止虐待兒童協會），協會旨在保障國內兒童的權益。

30. A - True 正確

By the end of World War II, Britain had amassed an immense debt of £21 billion. Much of this was held in foreign hands, with around £3.4 billion being owed overseas (mainly to creditors in the United States), a sum which represented around one third of annual GDP.

到二戰結束時，英國經已積累了 210 億英鎊的巨額債務，當中約 34 億英鎊為海外債務（美國為主要債權人）。

31. B - False 錯誤

The mission failed.

該殺人計劃失敗，未有炸死任何人。

32. B - False 錯誤

Arranged marriages, where both parties agree to the marriage, are acceptable in the UK.

在英國，由雙方同意的「包辦婚姻」為社會接受。

33. B - False 錯誤

Queen Elizabeth I was a Protestant, while her sister Mary I was a Catholic.

伊莉莎白一世是新教徒，其姊瑪麗一世則信奉天主教。

34. A - True 正確

Charles I wanted the worship of the Church of England to include more ceremony. He later introduced a revised Prayer Book.

查理一世希望令英格蘭教會的崇拜儀式變得更豐富，他後來對祈禱書作出增訂。

35. A - True 正確

大憲章保障了貴族的利益，並限制君主收稅、制訂或修改法律的權力。

36. A - True 正確

Walter Scott wrote poems inspired by Scotland and the traditional stories and songs from the area on the borders of Scotland and England.

華特·史葛的詩歌，靈感來自蘇格蘭以及蘇格蘭和英格蘭邊界地區的傳統故事和歌曲。

37. B - False 錯誤

The bell called Big Ben, housed in the Elizabeth Tower is over 150 years old and is a popular tourist attraction

位於伊莉莎白塔、名為「大本鐘」的旅遊景點，擁有超過 150 年的歷史。

38. A - True 正確

St. Patrick's Day is celebrated on March 17th as a holiday in the Republic of Ireland and a public holiday in Northern Ireland. If March 17th falls on a weekend, the following Monday will be a holiday in Northern Ireland.

3 月 17 日聖帕特里克節為愛爾蘭共和國和北愛爾蘭的公共假日。如果 3 月 17 日是周末，那麼下週一將是北愛爾蘭的假期。

39. A - True 正確

British values and principles are based on history and traditions and are protected by law, customs and expectations.

英國的價值觀和原則是以歷史和傳統為基礎，並受到法律、習俗和期望的保障。

40. B - False 錯誤

St. David is the patron saint of Wales and on 1st March is his feast day.

聖大衛是威爾斯的守護神，其節日是3月1日。

41. B - False 錯誤

The Laurence Olivier Awards take place annually at different venues in London.

「羅蘭士‧奧利花劇場頒獎禮」每年會於倫敦不同地方舉行。

42. B - False 錯誤

The Laurence Olivier Awards are named after the British actor Sir Laurence Olivier, later Lord Olivier, who was best known for his roles in various Shakespeare plays.

「羅蘭士‧奧利花劇場頒獎禮」以英國演員勞倫斯‧奧利維爾爵士（即後來的奧利維爾勳爵）的名字命名，他以在莎士比亞戲劇中的角色而聞名。

43. B - False 錯誤

Edward XI was the son of Henry VIII.

愛德華六世是亨利八世的兒子。

44. B - False 錯誤

Jane Seymour gave Henry VIII the son he wanted, Edward.

簡‧西摩給了亨利八世他想要的兒子，愛德華。

45. B - False 錯誤

It is a criminal offense to carry a weapon of any kind, even if it is for self-defense.

攜帶任何種類的武器都是刑事犯罪，即使是為了自衛。

46. B - False 錯誤

The Harrier jump jet, an aircraft capable of taking off vertically, was designed and developed in the UK.

獵鷹式戰鬥機（一種能夠垂直起飛的飛機）是在英國設計和開發。

47. A - True 正確

You can get a job and start to work even without a National Insurance number.

即使未獲發國民保險號碼，你仍可在英國找到工作。

48. A - True 正確

The Speaker of the House of Commons is neutral and does not represent a political party, even though he or she is an MP, represents a constituency and deals with the constituents' problems like any other MP.

英國的下議院議長地位中立，並不代表某個政黨，即使其本身屬國會議員，代表某個選區，並像任何其他國會議員一樣，負責處理選民的問題。

49. A - True 正確

When Cromwell died, his son Richard, became the Lord Protector in his place. However, Richard was not able to control the army or the government.

克倫威爾死後，兒子李察接替他成為護國公，但即使如此，卻仍然無法控制軍隊或政府。

50. B - False 錯誤

Elections helds in Britain at least every 5 years

英國全少每5年會舉行一次選舉。

51. A – True 正確

The UK is part of the United Nations.

英國是聯合國的一部分。

52. B – False 錯誤

Sir Francis Drake, one of the commanders in the defeat of the Spanish Armada.

弗朗西斯‧德雷克爵士是擊敗「西班牙無敵艦隊」的指揮官之一。

53. B - False 錯誤

Golden Hind was the ship of Sir Francis Drake

Golden Hind 是弗朗西斯‧德雷克爵士駕駛的船隻。

54. B – False 錯誤

The Union Flag has three crosses.

英國國旗上有3個交叉十字圖案。

55. A - True 正確

The devolved administrations each have their own civil service.

權力下放政府的行政部門，各有自己的公務員。

56. B - False 錯誤

In the UK, there is a National Lottery for which draws are made every tuesday and friday.

在英國，每週二和週五都會舉行國家彩票抽獎儀式。

57. A - True 正確

57. Anyone who is violent towards their partner – whether they are a man or a woman, married or living together – can be prosecuted.

任何對伴侶暴力的人——無論是男人還是女人，已婚還是同居——都可以被起訴。

58. B - False 錯誤

The Wimbledon Championships is the oldest tennis tournament in the world and the only 'Grand Slam' event played on grass.

溫布頓錦標賽是唯一在草地上進行的「大滿貫」賽事，也是世界上最歷史悠久的網球錦標賽。

59. A - True 正確

Habeas corpus is Latin for 'you must present the person in court'. The Habeas Corpus Act guaranteed that no one could be held prisoner unlawfully. Every prisoner has a right to a court hearing.

Habeas corpus 是拉丁語，意思是「你必須在法庭上出示任何人」，人身保護法保證任何人都不能被非法關押，每個囚犯都有權參加法庭聽證會。

60. B - False 錯誤

Hanukkah is in November or December and is celebrated for eight days. On each day of the festival a candle is lit on a stand of eight candles (called a menorah) to remember the story of the festival, where oil that should have lasted only a day did so for eight.

光明節在 11 或 12 月舉行，為期 8 天。在節日的每一天，一根蠟燭都會在「猶太教九燈燭台」（menorah）上點燃，以紀念節日的故事：原本應該只夠持續一天的燈油，竟奇蹟地用了 8 天。

61. B - False 錯誤

'The Enlightenment' is known as new ideas about politics, philosophy and science that were developed in the 18th century.

「啟蒙運動」是指在 18 世紀發展起來的關於政治、哲學和科學之新思想。

62. B - False 錯誤

Queen Elizabeth II borned on 21st April, 1926.

伊莉莎白二世生於 1926 年 4 月 21 日。

63. A - True 正確

During Halloween people carve lanterns out of Pumpkins and put a candle inside of them.

在萬聖節期間，人們會用南瓜雕刻燈籠，並在裡面放一支蠟燭。

64. B - False 錯誤

In 1801, Ireland became unified with England, Scotland and Wales after the Act of Union of 1800. This created the United Kingdom of Great Britain and Ireland.

1801 年，愛爾蘭在 1800 年聯合法案後與英格蘭、蘇格蘭和威爾斯統一。這創建了大不列顛及愛爾蘭聯合王國。

65. B – False 錯誤

Henry Purcell was the organist at Westminster Abbey. He wrote church music, operas and other pieces, and developed a British style distinct from that elsewhere in Europe.

亨利・珀塞爾是威斯敏斯特教堂的管風琴師。他創作了教堂音樂、歌劇和其他作品，並發展出一種不同於歐洲其他地方的英倫風格。

66. B – False 錯誤

Life peers are appointed by the monarch on the advice of the Prime Minister.

「終身貴族」是由君主根據首相的建議任命。

67. B - False 錯誤

The Giant's Causeway is located on the north-east coast of Northern Ireland.

巨人堤道位於北愛爾蘭的東北海岸。

2.3 正確項選擇(二選一)

Select the statement which you think is correct.

從兩個陳述中選擇一個你認為正確的選項。

1. **Which of the following statements is CORRECT?**

   以下哪個陳述是正確的？

   A. Ghana is not a member of the Commonwealth.

   加納不是英聯邦的成員國之一。

   B. Greece is not a member of the Commonwealth.

   希臘不是英聯邦的成員國之一。

2. **Which of the following statements is CORRECT?**

   以下哪個陳述是正確的？

   A. John Barbour was the first person in England to print books using a printing press.

   約翰・巴伯爾是英格蘭首位使用印刷機印書的人。

   B. William Caxton was the first person in England to print books using a printing press.

   威廉・卡克斯頓是英格蘭首位使用印刷機印書的人。

3. **Which of the following statements is CORRECT?**

   以下哪個陳述是正確的？

   A. The UK was the first signatory to The European Convention on Human Rights in 1940.

   英國是 1940 年《歐洲人權公約》的第一個簽署國。

   B. The UK was one of the first countries to sign the 'European Convention of Human Rights' in 1950.

   英國是 1950 年首批簽署《歐洲人權公約》的國家之一。

4. **Which of the following statements is CORRECT?**

   以下哪個陳述是正確的？

   A. The most famous rugby union competition is the 'All England Championship' between England, Ireland, Scotland, Wales, France and Italy.

   著名欖球賽事「全英錦標賽」，是由英格蘭、愛爾蘭、蘇格蘭、威爾斯、法國和意大利等國家競逐。

   B. The most famous rugby union competition is the 'Six Nations Championship' between England, Ireland, Scotland, Wales, France and Italy.

   著名欖球賽事「六國錦標賽」，是由英格蘭、愛爾蘭、蘇格蘭、威爾斯、法國和意大利等國家競逐。

5. **Which of the following statements is CORRECT?**

   以下哪個陳述是正確的？

   A. Hogmanay is an ancient festival and has roots in the pagan festival to mark the beginning of winter.

   霍格莫內（跨年）是一個起源於異教節日的古老節日，並紀念冬天的開始。

   B. Halloween is an ancient festival and has roots in the pagan festival to mark the beginning of winter.

   萬聖節是一個起源於異教節日的古老節日，並紀念冬天的開始。

6. **Which of the following statements is CORRECT?**

   以下哪個陳述是正確的？

   A. The Abolition Act abolished slavery throughout the British Empire.

   《廢除法案》廢除了整個大英帝國的奴隸制度。

   B. The Emancipation Act abolished slavery throughout the British Empire.

   《解放法案》廢除了整個大英帝國的奴隸制度。

7. **Which of the following statements is CORRECT?**

   以下哪個陳述是正確的？

   A. William Blake was inspired by nature.

   威廉・布克萊的（創作）靈感來自大自然。

   B. William Wordsworth was inspired by nature.

   威廉・華茲華斯的（創作）靈感來自大自然。

8. **Which of the following statements is CORRECT?**
   以下哪個陳述是正確的？

   A. The Equality Act 2010 incorporated the European Convention of Human Rights into UK law.
      《平等法 2010》將《歐洲人權公約》寫進英國法律。

   B. The Human Rights Act 1998 incorporated the European Convention of Human Rights into UK law.
      《人權法 1998》將《歐洲人權公約》寫進英國法律。

9. **Which of the following statements is CORRECT?**
   以下哪個陳述是正確的？

   A. The Scottish Grand National horse racing event is celebrated at Fife. It takcs place each year in April.
      每年四月，法夫都會舉行「蘇格蘭全國賽馬大賽」。

   B. The Scottish Grand National horse racing event is celebrated at Ayr. It takes place each year in April.
      每年四月，艾爾都會舉行「蘇格蘭全國賽馬大賽」。

10. **Which of the following statements is CORRECT?**

    以下哪個陳述是正確的？

    A. Oliver Cromwell was Prime Minister from 1945 to 1951 and led the Labor Party for 20 years.

    奧利弗‧克倫威爾於 1945 至 1951 年出任首相一職，並領導工黨 20 年。

    B. Clement Attlee was Prime Minister from 1945 to 1951 and led the Labor Party for 20 years.

    克萊門特‧艾德禮於 1945 至 1951 年出任首相一職，並領導工黨 20 年。

11. **Which of the following statements is CORRECT?**

    以下哪個陳述是正確的？

    A. South Downs is the highest mountain in Wales.

    南唐斯山是威爾斯最高的山峰。

    B. Snowdon is the highest mountain in Wales.

    斯諾登山是威爾斯最高的山峰。

12. **Which of the following statements is CORRECT?**

    以下哪個陳述是正確的？

    A. Local elections for councilors are held in March every year.

    地方議員選舉於每年三月舉行。

    B. Local elections for councilors are held in May every year.

    地方議員選舉於每年五月舉行。

13. **Which of the following statements is CORRECT?**

以下哪個陳述是正確的？

A. The Reform Act of 1832 had greatly increased the number of people with the right to vote. Also, it offered more parliamentary seats to the towns and cities.

《1832 年改革法案》除了令更多人可以投票外，更成功為城鎮爭取到不少議席。

B. The Reform Act of 1842 had greatly increased the number of people with the right to vote. Also, it offered more parliamentary seats to the towns and cities.

《1842 年改革法案》除了令更多人可以投票外，更成功為城鎮爭取到不少議席。

14. **Which of the following statements is CORRECT?**

以下哪個陳述是正確的？

A. Austria is a member of the Commonwealth.

奧地利是英聯邦的成員國。

B. Bangladesh is a member of the Commonwealth.

孟加拉是英聯邦的成員國。

15. **Which of the following statements is CORRECT?**

    以下哪個陳述是正確的？

    A. During the Crusades, European Christians fought for the control of the Holy Land.

       在十字軍東征期間，歐洲基督徒為控制聖地而戰。

    B. During the Crusades, European Christians fought for the control of Central Europe.

       在十字軍東征期間，歐洲基督徒為控制中歐而戰。

16. **Which of the following statements is CORRECT?**

    以下哪個陳述是正確的？

    A. The line 'To be or not to be' belongs to Shakespeare's play Romeo and Juliet.

       「To be or not to be」是莎士比亞戲劇《羅密歐與朱麗葉》的台詞。

    B. The line 'To be or not to be' belongs to Shakespeare's play Hamlet.

       「To be or not to be」是莎士比亞戲劇《哈姆雷特》的台詞。

17. **Which of the following statements is CORRECT?**

    以下哪個陳述是正確的？

    A. The Manhattan Project, led by Ernest Rutherford, produced the first atomic bomb.

    由歐內斯特・盧瑟福領導的「曼克頓計劃」，是一個專門研製原子彈的項目。

    B. The Michigan Project, led by Ernest Rutherford, produced the first atomic bomb.

    由歐內斯特・盧瑟福領導的「密歇根計劃」，是一個專門研製原子彈的項目。

18. **Which of the following statements is CORRECT?**

    以下哪個陳述是正確的？

    A. Most shops in the UK open seven days a week.

    英國的大多數商店每週七天營業。

    B. All shops in the UK close on Sundays and bank holidays.

    英國的所有商店都在週日和銀行假日關閉。

19. **Which of the following statements is CORRECT?**

    以下哪個陳述是正確的？

    A. MP is given to the members of the House of Commons.

    英國下議院議員的名字為 MP。

    B. MEP is given to the members of the House of Commons.

    英國下議院議員的名字為 MEP。

20. **Which of the following statements is CORRECT?**

    以下哪個陳述是正確的？

    A. It was before the 3rd century AD that the first Christian communities began to appear in Britain.

    英國在公元 3 世紀前，便出現第一個基督教社區。

    B. It was after the 13th century AD that the first Christian communities began to appear in Britain.

    英國在公元 13 世紀後，便出現第一個基督教社區。

21. **Which of the following statements is CORRECT?**

    以下哪個陳述是正確的？

    A. Edinburgh Castle is looked after by Historic Scotland.

    愛丁堡城堡由蘇格蘭文物局負責管理。

    B. Edinburgh Castle is looked after by The Scottish Parliament.

    愛丁堡城堡由蘇格蘭議會負責管理。

22. **Which of the following statements is CORRECT?**

    以下哪個陳述是正確的？

    A. Aneurin Bevan led the establishment of the National Health System (NHS) in 1948.

    安奈林・貝梵在 1948 年建立國民保健署。

    B. Harold Macmillan led the establishment of the National Health System (NHS) in 1948.

    哈羅德・麥克米倫在 1948 年建立國民保健署。

23. **Which of the following statements is CORRECT?**

以下哪個陳述是正確的？

A. Admiral Nelson's ship, HMS Victory, can be visited in Portsmouth.

你可以到樸茨茅夫，登上納爾遜海軍上將的「勝利號戰艦」參觀。

B. Admiral Nelson's ship, HMS Victory, can be visited in Plymouth.

你可以到普利茅夫，登上納爾遜海軍上將的「勝利號戰艦」參觀。

24. **Which of the following statements is CORRECT?**

以下哪個陳述是正確的？

A. The Puritans were a group of local leaders that surged in Wales with strict religious views

清教徒是一群以嚴格的宗教觀點湧入威爾斯的地方領袖。

B. The Puritans were a group of Protestants who advocated strict and simple religious doctrine and worship.

清教徒是一群主張嚴格而簡單的宗教教義和崇拜的新教徒。

25. **Which of the following statements is CORRECT?**

以下哪個陳述是正確的？

A. In the UK, some people rent additional land called 'Balcony', where they grow fruit and vegetables.

在英國，有些人會租用「天台」種植水果和蔬菜。

B. In the UK, some people rent additional land called 'Allotment', where they grow fruit and vegetables.

在英國，有些人會租用「社區農圃」種植水果和蔬菜。

26. **Which of the following statements is CORRECT?**

以下哪個陳述是正確的？

A. In 1314 the Scottish, led by Robert the Bruce, defeated the English at the Battle of Trafalgar.

在 1314 年，羅拔・布魯士帶領蘇格蘭軍隊，在特拉法加海戰中擊敗英國。

B. In 1314 the Scottish, led by Robert the Bruce, defeated the English at the Battle of Bannockburn.

在 1314 年，羅拔・布魯士帶領蘇格蘭軍隊，在班諾克本戰役中擊敗英國。

27. **Which of the following statements is CORRECT?**

以下哪個陳述是正確的？

A. Sir Christopher Cockerell, a British inventor, invented the hovercraft in the 1940s.

英國發明家克基斯杜化・科克雷爾爵士在 1940 年代發明氣墊船。

B. Sir Christopher Cockerell, a British inventor, invented the hovercraft in the 1950s.

英國發明家克基斯杜化・科克雷爾爵士在 1950 年代發明氣墊船。

28. **Which of the following statements is CORRECT?**

以下哪個陳述是正確的？

A. The London Eye is is a Ferris wheel about 443 feet (135 meters) tall.

倫敦眼是一座高 443 英呎（約 135 米）的摩天輪。

B. The London Eye is is a Ferris wheel about 135 feet (443 meters) tall.

倫敦眼是一座高 135 英呎（約 443 米）的摩天輪。

29. **Which of the following statements is CORRECT?**

以下哪個陳述是正確的？

A. Bonfire night is celebrated on October 5.

10 月 1 日為焰火節。

B. Bonfire night is celebrated on November 5.

11 月 5 日為焰火節。

30. **Which of the following statements is CORRECT?**

    以下哪個陳述是正確的？

    A. The Vikings first visited Britain in the year between 100 - 200 AD to raid coastal towns and take away goods and slaves.

    維京人於公元 100 至 200 年入侵英國，掠去沿海城鎮不少貨物和大量奴隸。

    B. The Vikings first visited Britain in the year between 700 - 800 AD to raid coastal towns and take away goods and slaves.

    維京人於公元 700 至 800 年入侵英國，掠去沿海城鎮不少貨物和大量奴隸。

31. **Which of the following statements is CORRECT?**

    以下哪個陳述是正確的？

    A. In Northern Ireland, policy and laws governing defense, foreign affairs, immigration, taxation and social security, are under the Irish government control.

    在北愛爾蘭，凡涉及國防、外交事務、移民、稅收和社會保障的政策和法律的事務，都是交由愛爾蘭政府控制。

    B. In Northern Ireland, policy and laws governing defense, foreign affairs, immigration, taxation and social security, are still under central UK government control.

    在北愛爾蘭，凡涉及國防、外交事務、移民、稅收和社會保障的政策和法律的事務，均仍然由英國中央政府控制。

32. **Which of the following statements is CORRECT?**

以下哪個陳述是正確的？

A. There are 12 national parks in England, Wales and Scotland.

英格蘭、威爾斯和蘇格蘭合計有 12 個國家公園。

B. There are 15 national parks in England, Wales and Scotland.

英格蘭、威爾斯和蘇格蘭合計有 15 個國家公園。

33. **Which of the following statements is CORRECT?**

以下哪個陳述是正確的？

A. In Northern Ireland, educational policy is under the devolved administrations control.

北愛爾蘭的教育事務，是由權力下放政府管理。

B. In Northern Ireland, educational policy is under central UK government control.

北愛爾蘭的教育事務，仍然由英國中央政府控制。

34. **Which of the following statements is CORRECT?**

以下哪個陳述是正確的？

A. 5% of the total British population is located in Scotland.

蘇格蘭佔英國總人口約 5 ％。

B. 8% of the total British population is located in Scotland.

蘇格蘭佔英國總人口約 8 ％。

35. **Which of the following statements is CORRECT?**
    以下哪個陳述是正確的？
    A. The Mercury Prize is the equivalent of the Oscars in the UK.
       水星獎的重要性相當於英國版奧斯卡電影金像獎。
    B. The BAFTA Awards are the equivalent of the Oscars in the UK.
       英國電影學院獎的重要性，相當於英國版奧斯卡電影金像獎。

36. **Which of the following statements is CORRECT?**
    以下哪個陳述是正確的？
    A. The Conservative Party was elected after the Second World War.
       保守黨在第二次世界大戰後當選。
    B. The Labor Party was elected after the Second World War.
       工黨在第二次世界大戰後當選。

37. **Which of the following statements is CORRECT?**
    以下哪個陳述是正確的？
    A. Sir Steve Redgrave was captain of the English cricket team.
       史蒂夫・雷德格雷夫爵士是英國板球隊隊長。
    B. Sir Ian Botham was captain of the English cricket team.
       伊恩・博瑟姆爵士是英國板球隊隊長。

38. **Which of the following statements is CORRECT?**

以下哪個陳述是正確的？

A. Edward VI died at the age of 15 after ruling for just over six years, and his half-sister Anne became queen.

愛德華六世在位六年多後，15 歲就去世了，他同父異母的妹妹安妮成為了王后。

B. Edward VI died at the age of 15 after ruling for just over six years, and his half-sister Mary became queen.

愛德華六世在位六年多後，15 歲就去世了，他同父異母的妹妹瑪麗成為了王后。

39. **Which of the following statements is CORRECT?**

以下哪個陳述是正確的？

A. Selling alcohol to anyone under the age of 18 is not classified as a criminal offense in the UK.

在英國，向 18 歲以下的任何人出售酒類，並不屬於刑事罪行。

B. Unfair dismissal or discrimination in the workplace is not classified as a criminal offense in the UK.

在英國，個人於工作場所遭不公平解僱或歧視，並不屬刑事罪行。

40. **Which of the following statements is CORRECT?**

以下哪個陳述是正確的？

A. The action of handing out leaflets in the street or knocking on people's doors to ask for their political support is known as 'Persuasion'.

在街上派發傳單或逐戶敲門尋求政治支持的行為，又稱為「說服」。

B. The action of handing out leaflets in the street or knocking on people's doors to ask for their political support is known as 'Canvassing'.

在街上派發傳單或逐戶敲門尋求政治支持的行為，又稱為「拉票」。

41. **Which of the following statements is CORRECT?**

以下哪個陳述是正確的？

A. King Alfred the Great defeated the Vikings.

阿爾弗雷德大帝打敗了維京人。

B. Boudicca defeated the Vikings.

布迪卡打敗了維京人。

42. **Which of the following statements is CORRECT?**

以下哪個陳述是正確的？

A. During the Middle Ages, England was an important trading nation and people came to England from abroad to trade and also to work. Canal builders came from Italy.

在中世紀，英國經已是一個重要的貿易國家，人們由外地到此貿易和工作，當中不少運河建設者都是來自意大利。

B. During the Middle Ages, England was an important trading nation and people came to England from abroad to trade and also to work. Canal builders came from Holland.

在中世紀，英國經已是一個重要的貿易國家，人們由外地到此貿易和工作，當中不少運河建設者都是來自荷蘭。

43. **Which of the following statements is CORRECT?**

以下哪個陳述是正確的？

A. Age UK is an organization that cares about the life of the elderly.

Age UK 是一個關注長者老後生活的服務機構。

B. Shelter is an organization that cares about the life of the elderly.

Shelter 是一個關注長者老後生活的服務機構。

44. **Which of the following statements is CORRECT?**

以下哪個陳述是正確的？

A. The modern game of football can be traced back to the 15th century in Scotland.

現代足球運動可以追溯到 15 世紀的蘇格蘭。

B. The modern game of golf can be traced back to the 15th century in Scotland.

現代高爾夫球運動可以追溯到 15 世紀的蘇格蘭。

45. **Which of the following statements is CORRECT?**

以下哪個陳述是正確的？

A. The suffragettes were a group who used 'civil disobedience' to gain the vote for women.

婦女參政運動者是一個透過公民抗命，爭取婦女投票權的組織。

B. The suffragettes were a group who demanded the vote for the working classes to gain power.

婦女參政運動者是一個要求投票給工人階級以獲得權力的團體。

46. **Which of the following statements is CORRECT?**
    以下哪個陳述是正確的？

    A. 'Ulster fry' is a fried meal from Northern Ireland with bacon, eggs, sausage, black pudding, tomatoes, mushrooms, soda bread and potato bread.

       「阿爾斯特煎」是來自北愛爾蘭的一種油炸食品，包括煙肉、雞蛋、香腸、黑布甸、蕃茄、蘑菇、蘇打麵包和馬鈴薯麵包。

    B. 'Sunday roast' is a fried meal from Northern Ireland with bacon, eggs, sausage, black pudding, tomatoes, mushrooms, soda bread and potato bread.

       「週日烤肉」是來自北愛爾蘭的一種油炸食品，包括煙肉、雞蛋、香腸、黑布甸、蕃茄、蘑菇、蘇打麵包和馬鈴薯麵包。

47. **Which of the following statements is CORRECT?**
    以下哪個陳述是正確的？

    A. The MP's office is located at The House of Lords, Westminster, London SW1A OAA.

       英國國會議員辦公室位於倫敦威斯敏斯特上議院 SW1A OAA。

    B. The MP's office is located at The House of Commons, Westminster, London SW1A OAA.

       英國國會議員辦公室位於倫敦威斯敏斯特下議院 SW1A OAA。

48. **Which of the following statements is CORRECT?**

以下哪個陳述是正確的？

A. The first tennis club was founded in Learnington Spa in 1772.

第一家網球俱樂部於 1772 年在利明頓斯帕成立。

B. The first tennis club was founded in Leamington Spa in 1872.

第一家網球俱樂部於 1872 年在利明頓斯帕成立。

49. **Which of the following statements is CORRECT?**

以下哪個陳述是正確的？

A. A 2 seconds' silence is observed on Remembrance Day.

在陣亡將士紀念日的悼念活動上，會有一個默哀 2 秒的儀式。

B. A 2 minutes' silence is observed on Remembrance Day.

在陣亡將士紀念日的悼念活動上，會有一個默哀 2 分鐘的儀式。

50. **Which of the following statements is CORRECT?**

以下哪個陳述是正確的？

A. In the Middle Ages, the numbers attending Parliament increased and two separate parts, known as Houses were established. These were the 'House of the Commons' and the 'House of the Lords'.

在中世紀，由於參加議會的人數增加，於是政府就將議會分為兩部分，亦即上議院和下議院。

B. In the The Roman Invasion, the numbers attending Parliament increased and two separate parts, known as Houses were established. These were the 'House of the Commons' and the 'House of the Lords'.

在羅馬征服不列顛時代，由於參加議會的人數增加，於是政府就將議會分為兩部分，亦即上議院和下議院。

51. **Which of the following statements is CORRECT?**

以下哪個陳述是正確的？

A. In the new Church of England created by Henry VIII, the King had the power to appoint bishops and order how people should worship.

在英王亨利八世創立的新英格蘭教會中，國王有權任命主教，並命令人們該如何進行禮拜。

B. In the new Church of England created by Henry VIII, the Pope had the power to appoint bishops and order how people should worship.

在英王亨利八世創立的新英格蘭教會中，教皇有權任命主教，並命令人們該如何進行禮拜。

52. **Which of the following statements is CORRECT?**

    以下哪個陳述是正確的？

    A. If you are self-employed, you need to pay your own tax through a system called EasyPay.

    自僱人士需通過一個名為「交稅易」的系統交稅。

    B. If you are self-employed, you need to pay your own tax through a system called Self-assessment.

    自僱人士需通過一個名為「自我評估」的系統交稅。

53. **Which of the following statements is CORRECT?**

    以下哪個陳述是正確的？

    A. William Shakespeare was born in Liverpool.

    威廉・莎士比亞出生於利物浦。

    B. William Shakespeare was born in Stratford-on-Avon.

    威廉・莎士比亞出生於埃文河畔斯特拉特福。

54. **Which of the following statements is CORRECT?**

    以下哪個陳述是正確的？

    A. Daffodil is the flower associated with Wales.

    水仙花與威爾斯有關。

    B. Shamrock is the flower associated with Wales.

    三葉草與威爾斯有關。

55. **Which of the following statements is CORRECT?**

以下哪個陳述是正確的？

A. In 1921 a peace treaty was signed and in 1922 Ireland became two countries.

1921 年簽署和平條約後，愛爾蘭在 1922 年分成兩個國家。

B. In 1921 a peace treaty was signed and in 1923 Ireland became two countries.

1921 年簽署和平條約後，愛爾蘭在 1923 年分成兩個國家。

56. **Which of the following statements is CORRECT?**

以下哪個陳述是正確的？

A. Henry VIII had six wives.

亨利八世有六個妻子。

B. Henry VIII had eight wives.

亨利八世有八個妻子。

2.3 Answers
答案及解題 (正確項選擇：二選一)

1. B

Greece is not a member of the Commonwealth.

希臘不是英聯邦的成員國之一。

2. B

William Caxton was the first person in England to print books using a printing press. And he also brought the technology of printing to England. Before Caxton set up his printing press in London, books in England were copied out by hand, by scribes.

威廉・卡克斯頓是英格蘭首位使用印刷機印書的人。除此之外，他更是將印刷技術帶到英國的人。在他的印刷公司（設於倫敦）成立前，英格蘭的書籍是由抄寫員用人手抄寫。

3. B

The Convention for the Protection of Human Rights and Fundamental Freedoms, better known as the European Convention on Human Rights, was signed in Rome on 4 November 1950 by 12 member states of the Council of Europe (including UK) and entered into force on 3 September 1953.

1950 年 11 月 4 日，包括英國在內的歐洲委員會 12 個成員國在意大利首都羅馬簽署《保護人權與基本自由公約》（即《歐洲人權公約》），公約於 1953 年 9 月 3 日生效。

4. B

England and Wales have won the championship the most times, both with 39 titles.

英格蘭在六國錦標賽奪冠次數和威爾斯並列首位，兩者均有 39 次封王的紀錄。

5. B

The spooky day associated with trick-or-treating and costumes of Halloween originates from Samhain, a three-day ancient Celtic pagan festival.

萬聖節的部份傳統習俗，例如穿上奇裝異服，挨家挨戶收集糖果，一般相信是源自古時凱爾特異教節日。

6. B

The Emancipation Act abolished slavery throughout the British Empire.

《解放法案》廢除了整個大英帝國的奴隸制度。

7. B

William Wordsworth was inspired by nature. Wordsworth repeatedly emphasizes the importance of nature to an individual's intellectual and spiritual development. A good relationship with nature helps individuals connect to both the spiritual and the social worlds. As Wordsworth explains in The Prelude, a love of nature can lead to a love of humankind.

威廉‧華茲華斯的創作靈感來自大自然。他反覆強調自然對個人智力和精神發展的重要性。與自然的良好關係，有助個人與精神世界和社會世界建立聯繫。正如他在自傳式長詩《序曲》中解釋，對自然的熱愛可以導致對人類的熱愛。

8. B

The Human Rights Act 1998 incorporated the European Convention of Human Rights into UK law.

《人權法 1998》將《歐洲人權公約》寫進英國法律。

9. B

The Scottish Grand National horse racing event is celebrated at Ayr. It takes place each year in April, over two days.

「蘇格蘭全國賽馬大賽」每年四月都會在艾爾舉行，賽事為期兩天。

10. B

Clement Attlee was Prime Minister from 1945 to 1951 and led the Labor Party for 20 years.

克萊門特‧艾德禮於 1945 至 1951 年出任首相，並領導工黨 20 年。

11. B

Snowdon Mountain, 1,085 meters above sea level and 1,038 meters above sea level, is the highest mountain in Wales and the second highest mountain in the UK.

斯諾登山，海拔 1,085 米，相對高度 1038 米。它是威爾斯的第一高山，英國的第二高山。

12. B

Local elections for councilors are held in May every year.

地方議員選舉於每年五月舉行。

13. A

There were 3 reforms in England: 1832, 1867 and 1884.

英格蘭曾進行過 3 次改革，分別為 1832 、1867 和 1884 年。

14. B

Bangladesh is a member of the Commonwealth.

孟加拉是英聯邦的成員國。

15. A

During the Crusades, European Christians fought for the control of the Holy Land.

在十字軍東征期間，歐洲基督徒為控制聖地而戰。

16. B

"To be, or not to be, that is the question." (from Hamlet, spoken by Hamlet).

哈姆雷特說：「生存還是毀滅，這是個問題。」（擇自威廉・莎士比亞戲劇《哈姆雷特》）。

17. A

The Manhattan Project was the codename for the American-led effort to develop a functional atomic weapon during World War II. Eventually 130,000 people participated in the Manhattan Project. By July 1945, scientists had developed three atomic bombs.

「曼克頓計劃」是第二次世界大戰期間，由美國領導的開發功能性原子武器的代號。計劃最終有 130,000 人參與。直至 1945 年 7 月，科學家們已經研製出三枚原子彈。

18. A

Most shops in the UK are open seven days a week, although trading hours on Sundays and public holidays are generally reduced.

英國的大多數商店每週七天營業，儘管週日和公共假日的營業時間通常會縮短。

19. A

'MP' stands for Member of Parliament, while 'MEP' refers to the Member of the European Parliament.

MP 代表國會議員的簡稱，至於 MEP 則是歐洲議會議員的英文縮寫。

20. A

It was before the 3rd century AD that the first Christian communities began to appear in Britain.

英國在公元 3 世紀前，便出現第一個基督教社區。

21. A

Historic Scotland is an agency of the Scottish Government responsible for the protection of Scotland's historic heritage. Currently, there are approximately 360 heritage sites in Scotland under the management and protection of the Authority.

蘇格蘭文物局是蘇格蘭政府一個機構，負責蘇格蘭的歷史遺產的保護工作。現時，蘇格蘭境內約有 360 座歷史遺產受該局管理和保護。

Following a motion in the Scottish Parliament in March 2014, the functions of Heritage Scotland were handed over to the Historic Environment Scotland, a non-government public body, in October 2015.

在 2014 年 3 月蘇格蘭議會一個議案，蘇格蘭文物局的職能於 2015 年 10 月移交給非政府部門公共機構「蘇格蘭歷史環境局」。

22. A

In 1948, Aneurin Bevan, the Minister for Health, led the establishment of the National Health Service (NHS), which guaranteed a minimum standard of health care for all, free at the point of use.

1948 年，衛生部長安奈林‧貝梵領導建立國民保健服務。該計劃保障民眾在使用醫療服務時，能免費享有最基本的醫療保健服務。

23. A

In 1922, HMS Victory was moved to a dry dock at Portsmouth, England, and preserved as a museum ship.

1922 年，勝利號戰艦被移至英國樸茨茅夫的乾船塢（用於船舶、船隻和其他船隻的建造、維護和修理），並作為一艘博物館船保存。

24. B

The Puritans did not agree with the king's religious views and disliked his reforms of the Church of England.

清教徒不同意國王的宗教觀點，不喜歡他對英國國教的改革。

25. B

Allotment, also known as community gardens or community gardens, are places for community residents to carry out gardening and farming. It encourages food security in urban communities, allowing residents to grow crops for themselves or donate to others.

「社區農圃」（又稱社區花園或社區園圃），旨在讓本區居民進行園藝與農事耕作的場地，讓租用人士可以種植作物自用，又或者捐贈他人。

26. B

Battle of Bannockburn, a decisive battle in Scottish history whereby the Scots under Robert I (the Bruce) defeated the English under Edward II, expanding Robert's territory and influence.

班諾克本戰役，乃蘇格蘭歷史上一場決定性的戰事，羅拔一世（羅拔·布魯士）領導下的蘇格蘭，擊敗了愛德華二世領導下的英國，擴大了前者的領土和影響力。

27. B

Sir Christopher Cockerell, a British inventor, invented the hovercraft in the 1950s.

英國發明家克基斯杜化·科克雷爾爵士在 1950 年代發明氣墊船。

28. A

The London Eye is situated on the southern bank of the River Thames, opposite the Houses of Parliament. It is a Ferris wheel about 443 feet (135 meters) tall.

倫敦眼位於泰晤士河南岸，與英國國會相對。它是一座高 443 英呎（約 135 米）的摩天輪。

29. B

Bonfire Night, November 5, is an occasion when people in Great Britain set off fireworks at home or in special displays.

11 月 5 日為焰火節（或「篝火之夜」），英國人通常會在家中或特殊表演中燃放煙花。

30. B

The Vikings first visited Britain in the year between 700 - 800 AD to raid coastal towns and take away goods and slaves.

維京人於公元 700 至 800 年侵襲英國，掠夫沿海城鎮不少貨物和大量奴隸。

31. B

In Northern Ireland, policy and laws governing defense, foreign affairs, immigration, taxation and social security, are still under central UK government control.

在北愛爾蘭，凡涉及國防、外交事務、移民、稅收和社會保障的政策和法律的事務，均仍然由英國中央政府控制。

32. B

There are 15 national parks in England, Wales and Scotland: 10 in England which cover 10% of the land area, three in Wales and two in Scotland.

英格蘭、威爾斯和蘇格蘭合計有 15 個國家公園：英格蘭有 10 個，威爾斯有 3 個，至於蘇格蘭則有 2 個。

33. A

In Northern Ireland, policy and laws governing defense, foreign affairs, immigration, taxation and social security, are still under central UK government control.
在北愛爾蘭，凡涉及國防、外交事務、移民、稅收和社會保障的政策和法律的事務，均仍然由英國中央政府控制。

However, many public services, such as education, are controlled by the devolved administrations.
不過，許多其他公共服務（如教育），則會交由權力下放政府的行政部門控制。

34. B

England makes up 84% of the total population 英格蘭佔總人口的 84％
Wales around 5% 威爾斯約佔 5％
Scotland just over 8% 蘇格蘭略多於 8％
Northern Ireland less than 3% 北愛爾蘭少於 3％

35. B

The BAFTA Awards are the equivalent of the Oscars in the UK.
英國電影學院獎的重要性，相當於英國版奧斯卡電影金像獎。

The Mercury Prize, formerly called the Mercury Music Prize, is an annual music prize awarded for the best album released in the United Kingdom by a British or Irish act.
水星獎（前稱「水星音樂獎」），是一項年度音樂獎，獎項將授予英國或愛爾蘭表演者在英國發行的最佳音樂專輯。

36. B

The Labor Party won the 1945 election. Clement Attlee was Prime Minister from 1945 to 1951 and led the Labor Party for 20 years.
工黨贏得 1945 年選舉。克萊門特‧艾德禮於 1945 至 1951 年擔任首相，並領導工黨 20 年。

37. B

Sir Ian Botham captained the English cricket team and holds a number of English Test Cricket records, while Sir Steve Redgrave is a British retired rower who won gold medals at five consecutive Olympic Games from 1984 to 2000.

伊恩‧博瑟姆爵士是英國板球隊隊長，擁有多項英國板球對抗賽的紀錄。至於史蒂夫‧雷德格雷夫爵士則是一位英國退役賽艇運動員，他在 1984 至 2000 年連續 5 屆奧運會上獲得金牌。

38. B

Mary I succeeded to the throne upon the death of her half-brother Edward VI, restoring the status of Roman Catholicism, replacing the Anglicanism advocated by her father Henry VIII during the Reformation in England. In the process, she ordered 300 dissidents to be burned to death, hence she was also nicknamed 'Bloody Mary'.

瑪麗一世於其同父異母弟弟愛德華六世死後繼承其王位，恢復羅馬天主教的地位，取代她父親亨利八世在英格蘭宗教改革提倡的新教盎格魯宗。過程中，她下令燒死300 名異見人士，故得名「血腥瑪麗」。

39. B

Unfair dismissal or discrimination in the workplace is not classified as a criminal offence in the UK.

在英國，個人於工作場所遭不公平解僱或歧視，並不屬刑事罪行。

40. B

The action of handing out leaflets in the street or knocking on people's doors to ask for their political support is known as 'Canvassing'.

在街上派發傳單或逐戶敲門尋求政治支持的行為，又稱為「拉票」。

41. A

King Alfred the Great defeated the Vikings.

阿爾弗雷德大帝打敗了維京人。

42. B

During the Middle Ages, England was an important trading nation and people came to England from abroad to trade and also to work. Canal builders came from Holland.

在中世紀，英國經已是一個重要的貿易國家，人們由外地到此貿易和工作，當中不少運河建設者都是來自荷蘭。

43. A

Age UK is a charity that works with old people, while Shelter is a charity that campaigns for tenant rights in Great Britain.

Age UK 是一個關注長者老後生活的服務機構，Shelter 則是一個致力為英國租戶爭取權利的慈善組織。

44. B

The modern game of golf can be traced back to the 15th century in Scotland.

現代高爾夫球運動可以追溯到 15 世紀的蘇格蘭。

45. A

The leader of the suffragettes in Britain, Emmeline Pankhurst is widely regarded as one of the most important figures in modern British history. She founded the Women's Social and Political Union (WSPU), a group known for employing militant tactics in their struggle for equality.

作為英國女權運動的領袖，艾米琳・潘克斯特被廣泛認為是英國現代歷史上最重要的人物之一。她創立了婦女社會政治聯盟，該組織以在爭取平等的過程中，採取激進手段聞名。

46. A

'Ulster fry' is a fried meal from Northern Ireland with bacon, eggs, sausage, black pudding, tomatoes, mushrooms, soda bread and potato bread, while The Sunday roast comprises beef, veggies and Yorkshire puds.

「阿爾斯特煎」（或稱阿爾斯特早餐）是來自北愛爾蘭的一種油炸食品，包括煙肉、雞蛋、香腸、黑布甸、蕃茄、蘑菇、蘇打麵包和馬鈴薯麵包。至於「週日烤肉」則包括牛肉、蔬菜和約克郡布甸。

47. B

The MP's office is located at The House of Commons, Westminster, London SW1A OAA.

英國國會議員辦公室位於倫敦威斯敏斯特下議院 SW1A OAA。

48. B

Beware of the spelling.

注意拼寫。

49. B

A 2 minutes' silence is observed on Remembrance Day.

在陣亡將士紀念日的悼念活動上，會有一個默哀 2 分鐘的儀式。

50. A

In the Middle Ages, the numbers attending Parliament increased and two separate parts, known as Houses were established. These were the 'House of the Commons' and the 'House of the Lords'.

在中世紀，由於參加議會的人數增加，於是政府就將議會分為兩部分，亦即上議院和下議院。

51. A

In the new Church of England created by Henry VIII, the King had the power to appoint bishops and order how people should worship.

在英王亨利八世創立的新英格蘭教會中，國王有權任命主教，並命令人們該如何進行禮拜。

52. B

If you are self-employed, you need to pay your own tax through a system called Self-assessment.

自僱人士需通過一個名為「自我評估」的系統交稅。

53. B

William Shakespeare was born in Stratford-upon-Avon, England, in April 1564. The exact date of his birth is not recorded, but it is most often celebrated around the world on 23 April.

威廉‧莎士比亞於 1564 年 4 月出生於英國埃文河畔斯特拉特福。他的確切出生日期雖然難以考證，但世界各地最常在 4 月 23 日慶祝。

54. A

The daffodil is considered the national flower of Wales and is traditionally worn by those who celebrate St David's Day.

水仙花被認為是威爾斯的國花，傳統上由慶祝聖大衛日的人士佩戴。

55. A

In 1921 a peace treaty was signed and in 1922 Ireland became two countries, which is called the Anglo-Irish Treaty.

1921 年簽署和平條約後，愛爾蘭在 1922 年分成兩國。該條約名為《英愛條約》。

56. A

Henry VIII had six wives: Catherine of Aragon, Anne Boleyn, Jane Seymour, Anne of Cleves, Catherine Howard and Katherine Parr.

亨利八世有六個妻子，她們分別為：阿拉貢的凱瑟琳、安妮‧博林、珍‧西摩、克萊沃的安娜、嘉芙蓮‧霍華德和嘉芙蓮‧帕爾。

2.4 多選題（四選二）

Select two correct answers from four options.
從四個選項中選擇兩個正確答案。您需要選擇兩個正確
答案才能對此類問題有所了解。

1. **During the 19th century, the UK was the world's major producer of the following materials: (Choose TWO)**
   在 19 世紀，英國是以下哪些材料的主要生產國？（選兩個）
   A. Coal　煤炭
   B. Iron　鐵
   C. Silk　絲綢
   D. Plastic　塑膠

2. **Which of the following British athletes have won gold medals in the Olympic Games? (Choose TWO)**
   以下哪些英國運動員曾奪奧運金牌？（選兩個）
   A. Dame Kelly Holmes　凱利・福爾摩斯夫人
   B. Jenson Button　簡森・巴頓
   C. Tim henman　蒂姆・亨曼
   D. Jessica Ennis　傑西卡・埃尼斯

3. **Which of the following are examples of criminal offenses? (Choose TWO)**

以下哪些行為屬於刑事罪行？（選兩個）

A. Unfair dismissal or discrimination in the workplace

於工作場所被不公平解僱或歧視

B. Selling tobacco to anyone under the age of 18

向 18 歲以下人士出售菸草

C. A dispute about faulty goods or services

出售損壞的商品或關於服務的爭議

D. Drinking in public places

於公共場所喝酒

4. **The job of the police in the UK is to: (Choose TWO)**

英國警察的職責包括：（選兩個）

A. Committ crimes　犯法

B. Not answering calls for help　不接聽求助電話

C. Protect life and property　保護生命和財產

D. Prevent and detect crime　預防和偵查犯罪

5. **Which of the following are core values of a civil servant? (Choose TWO)**

以下哪些是公務員的核心價值？（選兩個）

A. Objectivity　客觀

B. Competitiveness　競爭力

C. Talent　人才

D. Honesty　誠實

6. Which new industries developed in the UK during the Great Depression? (Choose TWO)

哪些行業在大蕭條時期乘勢而興？（選兩個）

A. Metallurgic industry　冶金業

B. Automobile industry　汽車業

C. Shipbuilding industry　造船業

D. Aviation industry　航空業

7. What does the money from the National Insurance Contributions pay for? (Choose TWO)

國民保險供款用於支付哪些費用？（選兩個）

A. Police force salaries　警隊薪金

B. State retirement pensions　國家退休金

C. National Health Service　國民保健服務

D. Build a luxury music fountain　興建豪華音樂噴水池

8. As a permanent resident or citizen of the UK, you should: (Choose TWO)

作為英國永久居民或公民，你需要：（選兩個）

A. Treat other with fairness　公平待人

B. Conquer people by force　以武服人

C. Look after the area in which you live and the environment
　　愛護自己居住的地區

D. All the answers are correct 所有答案都是正確的

9. **The development of the Bessemer process during the Industrial Revolution, led to the development of which two industries? (Choose TWO)**

在工業革命期間，貝塞麥法轉爐煉鋼法的發展，惠及哪些行業的發展？（選兩個）

A. Shipbuilding industry　造船業

B. Chemical industry　化工業

C. Railways industry　鐵路業

D. Car industry　汽車業

10. **Which of the following poems are from the Middle Ages? (Choose TWO)**

以下哪些是中世紀的詩？（選兩個）

A. The Canterbury Tales　坎特伯雷的故事

B. Paradise Lost　失樂園

C. Sir Gawain and the Green Knight　高文爵士與綠騎士

D. MacBeth　馬克白

11. **Where did the Vikings come from? (Choose TWO)**

維京人是來自哪些國家？（選兩個）

A. France 法國

B. Sweden 瑞典

C. Denmark 丹麥

D. Norway 挪威

12. **Which of the following are the principles included in the European Convention of Human Rights? (Choose TWO)**
以下哪些是《歐洲人權公約》入面，所包含的原則？（選兩個）

A. Resumption of executions　恢復執行死刑

B. Prohibition of immoral thoughts　禁止不道德的想法

C. Freedom of expression　表達自由

D. Prohibition of slavery and forced labour
禁止奴役和強迫勞動

13. **Some of the most well-known galleries are: (Choose TWO)**
英國有不少著名畫廊，例子有：（選兩個）

A. Tate Modern in London　泰特現代藝術館

B. the International Museum in Cardiff　卡迪夫國際博物館

C. the Timeout Art Gallery in Leeds　利茲的 Timeout 藝術畫廊

D. Tate Britain　泰特不列顛

14. **Who were the pioneers of IVF (In-vitro fertilization) therapy? (Choose TWO)**
誰是體外受精療法先驅？（選兩個）

A. Sir Frank Whittle　弗蘭克・惠特爾爵士

B. Sir Robert Edwards　羅拔・愛德華茲爵士

C. Patrick Steptoe　帕特里克・斯特普托

D. Sir Ian Wilmot　伊恩・威爾莫特爵士

15. **Which of the following countries were granted their independence in 1947? (Choose TWO)**

    以下哪些國家在 1947 年獨立？（選兩個）

    A. India　印度

    B. Bangladesh　孟加拉

    C. Pakistan　巴基斯坦

    D. British Malaya　英屬馬來亞

16. **Which of the following are British poets of the 19th century? (Choose TWO)**

    以下哪些是 19 世紀的英國詩人？（選兩個）

    A. William Blake　威廉・布萊克

    B. John Keats　約翰・濟慈

    C. Ted Hughes　特德・休斯

    D. Philip Larkin　菲臘・拉金

17. **Which of the following are the roles of the King? (Choose TWO)**

    以下哪些是國王的職責？（選兩個）

    A. To inaugurate important business in the UK
       在英國開展重要業務

    B. To receive foreign ambassadors and high commissioners
       接待外國大使和高級專員

    C. To entertain visiting heads of state　招待來訪的國家元首

    D. All of the above 以上皆是

18. **Governors and school boards have an important part to play in raising school standards, they have three key roles: (Choose TWO)**

地方行政長官和學校董事會在提高學校水平，扮演著重要的角色，它們主要負責：（選兩個）

A. setting the strategic direction of the school
   確定學校的戰略方向

B. monitoring the students so they go direct to home
   監控學生，確保他們直接回家

C. ensuring accountability　確保問責制

D. setting the benches for all the students
   所有學生設置長椅

19. **Some of the principles included in the European Convention on Human Rights are: (Choose TWO)**

《歐洲人權公約》列明：（選兩個）

A. right to life　生存的權利

B. right to fight　戰爭的權利

C. prohibition of slavery and forced labour
   禁止奴役和強迫勞動

D. prohibition of speech　禁止言論

20. **In which Japanese cities did the United States drop atomic bombs in August 1945? (Choose TWO)**
1945 年 8 月，美國向哪些日本城市投擲原子彈？（選兩個）
A. Tokyo　東京
B. Osaka　大阪
C. Hiroshima　廣島
D. Nagasaki　長崎

21. **What is a bank holiday? (Choose TWO)**
什麼是銀行假期？（選兩個）
A. A festive pagan day　異教節日
B. A private holiday　私人假期
C. A day when banks are closed　銀行會於這天關門
D. A public holiday　公眾假期

22. **A Formula 1 Grand Prix event is held in the UK each year and a number of British Grand Prix drivers have won the Formula 1 World Championship. Recent British winners include Damon Hill, _____ and _____ . (Choose TWO)**
每年的一級方程式大賽車都會在英國舉行，英國許多一級方程式車手都曾贏得賽事的世界冠軍。最近的英國獲獎者包括達蒙·希爾、_____ 和 _____ 。（選兩個）
A. Lewis Hamilton　劉易斯·咸美頓
B. Jensen Button　贊神·巴頓
C. George William Russell　喬治·威廉·羅素
D. Lando Norris　蘭多·諾里斯

23. **Which of the following are 'Crown dependencies'? (Choose TWO)**

以下哪些是皇室屬地？（選兩個）

A. The Maldives　馬爾代夫

B. Anglesey　安格爾西島

C. The Isle of Man　馬恩島（或稱曼島）

D. Bailiwick of Jersey　澤西島轄區

24. **Which of the following are cities of England? (Choose TWO)**

以下哪些是英格蘭的城市？（選兩個）

A. Bath　巴斯

B. Armagh　阿馬郡

C. Dublin　都柏林

D. Carlisle　卡萊爾

25. **Which of the following countries are members of the Commonwealth? (Choose TWO)**

以下哪些是英聯邦的成員國？（選兩個）

A. Uganda　烏干達

B. Ghana　加納

C. Greece　希臘

D. Zimbabwe　津巴布韋

26. **Anyone can make a complaint about the police by: (Choose TWO)**

    任何人均可通過以下方式投訴警方：（選兩個）

    A. visiting the local polling places　前往地區票站

    B. going to a police station　到警局

    C. visiting a council office　到議會辦公室

    D. writing to the Chief Constable of the police force involved
    寫信給警察總長

27. **The structure of the DNA molecule was discovered in 1953 through work at British universities in _____ and _____. This discovery contributed to many scientific advances, particularly in medicine and fighting crime. (Choose TWO)**

    DNA 分子結構是 1953 年通過在_____和_____的英國大學的研究成果，該發現亦促進其他方面的發展，特別是醫學和打擊犯罪。（選兩個）

    A. Cambridge　劍橋

    B. Portsmouth　樸茨茅夫

    C. London　倫敦

    D. Plymouth　普利茅夫

28. **The television was developed by Scotsman John Logie Baird in the 1920s. In 1932 he made the first television broadcast between _____ and _____ . (Choose TWO)**

   電視是由蘇格蘭人約翰・洛吉・貝爾德在 1920 年代發明。在 1932 年，他在_____ 和 _____之間進行了第一次電視廣播。（選兩個）

   A. London　倫敦

   B. Liverpool　利物浦

   C. Glasgow　格拉斯哥

   D. Birmingham　伯明翰

29. **The job of the police in the UK is to: (Choose TWO)**

   英國警察的職責是：（選兩個）

   A. protect life and property　保護生命和財產

   B. protect the trees　保護樹木

   C. prevent disturbances and keeping the peace
   防止社會混亂，並維持社會治安

   D. prevent floods　防洪

30. **In the north of _____, land was owned by members of the 'Clans' (prominent families)**

(Choose TWO)

英國哪些地方的北部是歸氏族（顯赫家族）擁有？（選兩個）

A. England　英格蘭

B. Scotland　蘇格蘭

C. Ireland　愛爾蘭

D. Wales　威爾斯

31. **Which of the following are public holidays? (Choose TWO)**

以下哪些是公眾假期？（選兩個）

A. Good Friday　聖週五

B. April Fool's Day　愚人節

C. Easter Monday　復活節星期一

D. St. Valentine's Day　情人節

32. **The Parliament developed in Scotland in the Middle Ages had three Houses: the House of Lords, _____ and _____.**

(Choose TWO)

在中世紀，蘇格蘭將議會分為上議院、_____和_____。（選兩個）

A. The House of Commons　下議院

B. The farmers　農民

C. The Clergy　神職人員

D. The blacksmiths　鐵匠

33. **What is the money raised from the income tax used for? (Choose TWO)**

政府將所得稅的稅款用於哪方面？（選兩個）

A. Education 教育

B. The National Grid system 國家電網系統

C. Investment 投資

D. Roads 道路

34. **Which of the following are World Heritage Sites? (Choose TWO)**

以下哪些著名景點屬於世界遺產？（選兩個）

A. The London Eye 倫敦眼

B. Stonehenge 巨石陣

C. The forts of Housesteads and Vindolanda
豪斯泰德和文多蘭達堡壘

D. Buckingham Palace 白金漢宮

35. **People in the UK have to pay tax on any earnings from: (Choose TWO)**

在英國，個人必須就以下入息交稅：（選兩個）

A. Profits in self-employment 從自僱工作賺到的工資

B. Income from property, savings and dividends
財產、儲蓄和股息收益

C. Valuable gifts 貴重禮物

D. All of the above 以上皆是

36. **In which of the following areas has the Welsh Assembly the power to make laws? (Choose TWO)**

    威爾斯議會有權就下列哪些範圍制定法律？（選兩個）

    A. Education and training　教育和培訓

    B. Military defence　軍事防禦

    C. Economic development　經濟發展

    D. Immigration　移民

37. **What names are given to the people who give tours at the Tower of London? (Choose TWO)**

    在倫敦塔向遊客介紹該座歷史塔的人，又稱為：（選兩個）

    A. Beefeaters　衛兵（或食牛肉者）

    B. Suffragettes　參政者

    C. Chartists　憲章主義者

    D. Yeoman Warders　倫敦塔御用侍從衛士

38. **The European Union member states are: (Choose TWO)**

    歐盟的成員國包括：（選兩個）

    A. Germany　德國

    B. India　印度

    C. Lithuania　立陶宛

    D. Nigeria　尼日利亞

    E. New Zealand　新西蘭

39. **Henry VIII was most famous for: (Choose TWO)**

亨利八世最廣為人知的事情為： (選兩個)

A. breaking away from the Church of Rome 脫離羅馬教會

B. bringing peace to the UK 為英國帶來和平

C. marrying six times 結婚六次

D. his great skills of art 高超的藝術技巧

40. **Which of the following is a traditional food from Northern Ireland? (Choose TWO)**

以下哪項是北愛爾蘭的傳統食品？ (選兩個)

A. Roast beef 烤牛肉

B. Haggis 哈吉斯

C. Yellow man 黃人

D. Ulster fry 阿爾斯特早餐

41. **People in the UK have to pay tax on their income, which includes: (Choose TWO)**

英國人須就收入納稅，包括： (選兩個)

A. Disability Living Allowance 殘疾生活津貼

B. Profits from self-employment 自僱工作的利潤

C. Income from property, savings and dividends
財產、儲蓄和股息收入

D. Working / Child Tax Credit 工作 / 兒童稅收豁免

42. **In the mid-19th century, the Chartists campaigned for democratic reforms including: (Choose TWO)**

在 19 世紀中葉，憲章派運動的民主改革包括：（選兩個）

A. All women to have the vote　所有女性都有投票權

B. MPs to be paid　國會議員均會獲得薪酬

C. Any man to be able to stand as an MP

任何人都可以出任國會議員

43. **Which of the following are famous horse racing events in the UK? (Choose TWO)**

以下哪些是英國著名的賽馬賽事？（選兩個）

A. The Major Race　主要賽事

B. Epsom Derby　葉森打吡大賽

C. Cheltenham Festival　切爾滕納姆節

D. Six Nations Championship　六國錦標賽

44. **_____ is England's largest national park, while the smallest one is _____ . (Choose TWO)**

_____是英格蘭面積最大的國家公園，而_____則是英格蘭面積最小的國家公園。（選兩個）

A. The Lake District　湖區

B. Snowdonia　斯諾登尼亞

C. The New Forest　新森林國家公園

D. Loch Lomond and the Trossachs　洛蒙德湖和特羅薩克斯

45. **Which of the following films were directed by Christopher Nolan? (Choose TWO)**

基斯杜化・路蘭曾執導哪些電影？（選兩個）

A. Interstellar 《星際啟示錄》

B. The 39 Steps 《國防大機密》

C. Lawrence of Arabia 《沙漠梟雄》

D. Following 《跟蹤》

46. **The UK has hosted the Olympic games in 1908, _____ and _____ . (Choose TWO)**

英國於 1908、_____和_____年舉辦過奧運會。（選兩個）

A. 1936

B. 1948

C. 1952

D. 2012

47. **Which of the following persons were famous Victorians? (Choose TWO)**

以下哪些是英國在維多利亞時代的著名人物？（選兩個）

A. Dylan Thomas 狄蘭・湯瑪斯

B. Florence Nightingale 弗羅倫斯・南丁格爾

C. Isambard Kingdom Brunei 伊桑巴德・金德姆・布魯內爾

D. Margaret Thatcher 戴卓爾夫人

48. The English Civil Wars occurred from 1642 through 1651. The fighting during this period is traditionally broken into three wars: the first happened from 1642 to 1646, the second in _____, and the third from _____ to 1651. (Choose TWO)

英國內戰發生於 1642 至 1651 年，該戰爭一般被分為三個階段：首階級在 1642 至 1646 年；第二階段在_____年；第三次則在_____至 1651 年。（選兩個）

A. 1647

B. 1648

C. 1649

D. 1650

49. The most famous architectural buildings in the UK include: (Choose TWO)

英國的著名建築包括：（選兩個）

A. St. Paul's Cathedral　聖保羅大教堂

B. Lincoln Cathedral　林肯大教堂

C. Cologne Cathedral　科隆大教堂

D. Empire State Building　帝國大廈

50. **Which of the following cities are in Wales? (Choose TWO)**

以下哪些城市位於威爾斯？（選兩個）

A. St. Asaph　聖阿薩夫

B. Bangor　班戈

C. Nottingham　諾定咸

D. London　倫敦

2.4 Answers
答案及解題 (多選題：四選二)

1. A, B

British industry led the world in the 19th century. The UK produced more than half of the world's iron, coal and cotton cloth.

英國工業在 19 世紀引領全球，國內生產世界一半以上的煤炭、鐵和棉布。

2. A, D

Dame Kelly Holmes won two gold medals for running in the 2004 Olympic Games. She has held a number of British and European records.

凱利・福爾摩斯夫人在 2004 年奧運會上獲得兩面賽跑金牌。她擁有多項英國和歐洲賽紀錄。

Jessica Ennis won the 2012 Olympic gold medal in the heptathlon, which includes seven different track and field events. She also holds a number of British athletics records.

傑西卡・埃尼斯贏得 2012 年奧運會七項全能金牌，其中包括七項不同的田徑項目。她還擁有多項英國田徑紀錄。

3. B, D

- Selling tobacco: it is illegal to sell tobacco products (for example, cigarettes, cigars, roll-up tobacco) to anyone under the age of 18.

出售菸草：向 18 歲以下的任何人出售菸草製品（例如香煙、雪茄、捲菸）是違法的。

- Drinking in public: some places have alcohol-free zones where you cannot drink in public.

在公共場所飲酒：有些地方設有禁酒區，故在公共場所隨便飲酒就有可能會觸犯法例。

4. C, D

The job of the police in the UK is to protect life and property, keeping the peace and prevent and detect crime

英國警察的職責是：保護生命和財產、維護和平和預防和偵查犯罪。

5. A, D

The core values of civil servants include: integrity, honesty, objectivity and impartiality (including being politically neutral).

公務員的核心價值包括：正直、誠實、客觀和公正（包括政治中立）。

6. B, D

In 1929, the world entered the 'Great Depression' and some parts of the UK suffered mass unemployment. Traditional heavy industries, for example, shipbuilding were badly affected but new industries – including the automobile and aviation industries – developed.

1929 年，世界進入「大蕭條」格局，英國失業問題嚴重。一些傳統的重工業（如造船）遭受嚴重影響。不過，一些新興行業如汽車業、航空業卻異軍突起。

7. B, C

The money raised from National Insurance Contributions is used to pay for state benefits and services such as the state retirement pension and the National Health Service (NHS).

英國政府會將從國民保險繳款中籌集得來的資金，用於支付國家福利和服務等經費，例如國家退休金和國民健康服務。

8. A, C

If you wish to be a permanent resident or citizen of the UK, you should: respect and obey the law, respect the rights of others, including their right to their own opinions, treat others with fairness, look after yourself and your family and look after the area in which you live and the environment.

如果你希望成為英國永久居民或公民，便應當：尊重和遵守法律、尊重別人的權利（包括發表意見的權利）、公平待人、好好照顧自己和家人，以及愛護自己居住的地區。

9. A, C

The development of the Bessemer process for the mass production of steel led to the development of the shipbuilding industry and the railways.

大規模生產鋼鐵的貝塞麥法轉爐煉鋼法之發展，導致造船業和鐵路業的萌芽。

10. A, C

The Canterbury Tales and Sir Gawain and the Green Knight were poems from the Middle Ages.

《坎特伯雷的故事》和《高文爵士與綠騎士》是中世紀的詩作。

11. C, D

Vikings came Denmark and Norway

維京人來自丹麥和挪威。

12. C, D

Prohibition of immoral thoughts and resumption of executions are not one of the principles included in the European Convention of Human Rights.

禁止不道德的思想和恢復執行死刑，並沒有寫在歐洲人權公約中包含的原則之中。

13. A, D

Some of the most well-known galleries are: Tate Modern in London and Tate Britain.

英國有不少著名畫廊，例如：泰特現代藝術館和泰特不列顛。

14. B, C

IVF (in-vitro fertilization) therapy for the treatment of infertility was pioneered in Britain by physiologist Sir Robert Edwards and gynecologist Patrick Steptoe. The world's first 'test-tube baby' was born in Oldham, Lancashire in 1978.

生理學家羅拔‧愛德華茲爵士和婦科醫生帕特里克‧斯特普托在英國開創使用於治療不孕症的 IVF（體外受精）療法。世界上第一個「試管嬰兒」於 1978 年於蘭開夏郡的奧爾德姆出生。

15. A, C

In 1947, independence was granted to nine countries, including India, Pakistan and Ceylon (now Sri Lanka).

1947 年，印度、巴基斯坦和錫蘭（現斯里蘭卡）等九個國家獨立。

16. A, B

Poetry was very popular in the 19th century, with poets such as William Blake, John Keats, Lord Byron, Percy Shelley, Alfred Lord Tennyson, and Robert and Elizabeth Browning.

詩歌在 19 世紀的英國非常流行，著名詩人包括：威廉・布萊克 / 約翰・濟慈 / 拜倫勳爵 / 珀西・雪萊 / 阿爾弗雷德・丁尼生勳爵 / 羅拔 / 伊莉莎白・布朗寧。

17. B, C

The King receives foreign ambassadors and high commissioners, entertains visiting heads of state, and makes state visits overseas in support of diplomatic and relationships with other countries.

國王接待外國大使和高級專員，招待來訪的國家元首，並到外國進行國事訪問，以支持與其他國家的外交和關係。

18. A, C

Governors and school boards have an important part to play in raising school standards, they have three key roles, such as: setting the strategic direction of the school and ensuring accountability.

地方行政長官和學校董事會在提高學校水平，扮演著重要的角色，它們主要負責確定學校的戰略方向，並確保問責制。

19. A, C

The right to life and prohibition of slavery and forced labor are principles included in the European Convention on Human Rights.

《歐洲人權公約》列明我們有生存的權利，公約並列明禁止奴役和強迫勞動。

20. C, D

The war against Japan ended in August 1945 when the United States dropped its newly developed atom bombs on the Japanese cities of Hiroshima and Nagasaki.

隨著美國向日本廣島和長崎市在 1945 年 8 月投擲新研製的原子彈，事件令對日戰爭宣告結束。

21. C, D

In the UK, there are public holidays each year called bank holidays, when banks and many other businesses are closed for the day.

在英國，每年都有「銀行假期」，銀行和許多公司都不會在這天辦公。

22. A, B

A Formula 1 Grand Prix event is held in the UK each year and a number of British Grand Prix drivers have won the Formula 1 World Championship. Recent British winners include Damon Hill, Lewis Hamilton and Jensen Button.

每年的一級方程式大賽車都會在英國舉行，英國許多一級方程式車手都曾贏得賽事的世界冠軍。最近的英國獲獎者包括達蒙・希爾、劉易斯・咸美頓和贊神・巴頓。

23. C, D

The Crown Dependencies are the Bailiwick of Jersey, the Bailiwick of Guernsey and the Isle of Man.

Within the Bailiwick of Guernsey there are three separate jurisdictions: Guernsey (which includes the islands of Herm and Jethou); Alderney; and Sark (which includes the island of Brecqhou).

皇室屬地包括澤西島轄區、馬恩島和根西島轄區。後者又分為三個獨立的司法管轄區：根西島（包括赫姆島和傑圖島）、奧爾德尼島和 Sark（包括 Brecqhou 島）。

24. A, D

Bath is located in the south west of England, while Carlisle is in the north west of England.

巴斯位於英格蘭的西南面，卡萊爾則位於英格蘭的西北面。

25. A, B

Uganda and Ghana are members of the Commonwealth.

烏干達和加納都是英聯邦的成員國。

26. B, D

Anyone can make a complaint about the police by going to a police station and writing to the Chief Constable of the police force involved.

任何人均可通過親身到警局或寫信給警察總長投訴警方。

27. A, C

The structure of the DNA molecule was discovered in 1953 through work at British universities in London and Cambridge. This discovery contributed to many scientific advances, particularly in medicine and fighting crime.

DNA 分子的結構是 1953 年通過在倫敦和劍橋的英國大學的研究工作發現的。這一發現促進了其他方面的發展,特別是在醫學和打擊犯罪方面。

28. A, C

The television was developed by Scotsman John Logie Baird in the 1920s. In 1932 he made the first television broadcast between London and Glasgow.

電視是由蘇格蘭人約翰‧洛吉‧貝爾德在 1920 年代發明。在 1932 年,他在倫敦和格拉斯哥之間進行首次電視廣播。

29. A, C

The job of the police in the UK is to protect life and property and prevent disturbances and keep the peace.

英國警察的職責包括保護生命和財產,以及防止社會混亂,並維持社會治安。

30. B, C

In the north of Scotland and Ireland, land was owned by members of the 'Clans' (prominent families).

蘇格蘭和愛爾蘭的北部是歸氏族(顯赫家族)擁有。

31. A, C

Good Friday and Easter Monday are public holidays.

聖週五和復活節星期一為英國的公眾假期。

32. A, C

The Parliament developed in Scotland in the Middle Ages had three Houses: the House of Lords, the House of Commons and the Clergy.

在中世紀時期，蘇格蘭議會分三個，包括：上議院、下議院和神職人員。

33. A, D

Money raised from income tax pays for government services such as roads, education, police and the armed forces.

英國政府從所得稅項中籌集的資金，將用於支付政府服務，例如道路、教育、警察和武裝部隊等。

34. B, C

The London Eye and Buckingham Palace are not World Heritage Sites.

倫敦眼和白金漢宮都沒被列入「世界遺產」的名單之內。

35. A, B

People in the UK have to pay tax on their income, which includes: wages from paid employment, profits from self-employment, taxable benefits, pensions and income from property, savings and dividends.

英國人必須為其收入納稅，包括：有償工作的工資、自僱所賺取的利潤、應稅福利、養老金和財產收入、儲蓄和股息。

36. A, C

The Welsh Assembly has the power to make laws in 20 areas, including: education and training, health and social services, economic development and housing.

威爾斯議會有權在 20 個領域制定法律，包括：教育和培訓、衛生和社會服務、經濟發展和住房等。

37. A, D

Tours to the Tower of London are given by the Yeoman Warders, also known as Beefeaters, who tell visitors about the building's history.

「倫敦塔之旅」由倫敦塔御用侍從衛士（也稱為「食牛肉者」）提供，他們會為遊客介紹這座建築的歷史。

Henry VII's personal guards were the first 'Beefeaters', so named as they were permitted to eat as much beef as they wanted from the King's table, and Henry VIII decreed that some of them would stay and guard the Tower permanently.

亨利七世的貼身守衛是第一批「守衛者」，之所以如此命名，是因為他們被允許從國王的餐桌上吃多少牛肉就吃多少。後來，亨利八世下令讓他們中的一些人，留下來永久守衛塔樓。

38. A, C

The European Union member states are Germany and Lithuania.

歐盟的成員國包括德國和立陶宛。

39. A, C

Henry VIII was most famous for breaking away from the Church of Rome and marrying six times.

亨利八世最廣為人知的事情為脫離羅馬教會，並結婚六次。

40. C, D

Ulster fry – a fried meal with bacon, eggs, sausage, black pudding, tomatoes, mushrooms, soda bread and potato bread – is a traditional food from Northern Ireland.

「阿爾斯特早餐」是來自北愛爾蘭的傳統食物，入面有煙肉、雞蛋、香腸、黑布甸、蕃茄、蘑菇、蘇打麵包和馬鈴薯麵包的油炸食品。

'Yellow man' is a toffee, or honeycomb-like confection, which is a traditional candy of Northern Ireland made during Lammas, a harvest festival.

「黃人」則是一種太妃糖或蜂窩狀的糖果，是北愛爾蘭的傳統糖果，通常會在拉馬斯節（或稱收穫節）期間製作。

41. B, C

People in the UK have to pay tax on their income, which includes profits from self-employment and income from property, savings and dividends.

英國人須就收入納稅,包括自僱工作的利潤和財產、儲蓄和股息收入。

42. B, C

In the mid-19th century, the Chartists campaigned for democratic reforms including MPs to be paid. Also, any man to be able to stand as an MP.

在 19 世紀中葉,憲章派運動的民主改革包括國會議員均會獲得薪酬,以及任何人都可以出任國會議員。

43. B, C

Epsom Derby is usually held on June each year, while Cheltenham Festival is in March.

葉森打吡大賽於每年 6 月舉行,切爾滕納姆節則在 3 月上演。

44. A, C

The Lake District is England's largest national park. The whole Lake District National Park covers an area of 884.9 square miles (2,292 square Kilometers), while the smallest of the UK's national parks is the New Forest which covers only 570 square kilometers across Hampshire and Wiltshire.

湖區是英格蘭最大的國家公園,佔地 884.9 平方英里(2,292 平方公里),至於新森林國家公園的面積則最小,僅 570 平方公里,橫跨漢普郡和威爾特郡。

45. A, D

Following (1998) and Interstellar (2014) were directed by Christopher Nolan.

基斯杜化・路蘭曾於 1998 年和 2014 年執導電影《跟蹤》和《星際啟示錄》。

46. B, D

The UK has hosted the Olympic games on three occasions: 1908, 1948 and 2012.

英國曾舉辦過 3 屆奧運會,時間分別為 1908、1948 和 2012 年。

47. B, C

The Victorian era in England is usually defined as the period from 1837 to 1901, the reign of Queen Victoria.

英國的維多利亞時代，通常被定義為 1837 至 1901 年，即維多利亞女皇的統治時期。

48. B, D

The English Civil Wars occurred from 1642 through 1651.

The fighting during this period is traditionally broken into three wars: the first happened from 1642 to 1646, the second in 1648, and the third from 1650 to 1651.

英國內戰發生於 1642 至 1651 年，這場戰事傳統上被分為三個階段：首階級在 1642 至 1646 年；第二階段在 1648 年；第三次則在 1650 至 1651 年。

49. A, B

The most famous architectural buildings in the UK include St. Paul's Cathedral and Lincoln Cathedral.

英國的著名建築包括聖保羅大教堂和林肯大教堂。

50. A, B

Six cities in Wales: Bangor, Cardiff, Newport, St Asaph, St Davids and Swansea.

威爾斯的六個主要城市為：班戈、加的夫、紐波特、聖阿薩夫、聖戴維斯和史雲斯。

Chapter 3

模 擬 試 卷
Mock Papers

3.1 Mock Paper 1

The test consists of 24 questions, and you need to answer at least 18 correctly to pass.

1. The settlements of Scottish and English Protestants in Ulster (the northern province of Ireland) during the reigns of Elizabeth I and James I, who took over the land from Catholic landholders is known as:

    A. Plantations

    B. Cavaliers

    C. Puritans

    D. Pale

2. Who is the fastest person to have sailed around the world with just a single hand?

    A. Dame Kelly Holmes

    B. Dame Ellen MacArthur

    C. Jayne Torvill

    D. Bradley Wiggins

3. Which character is usually in a pantomime?

    A. The gentleman

    B. The Dame

    C. A unicorn

    D. A mermaid

4. **During the Wars of the Roses, what was the symbol of Lancaster?**

   A. Red Rose

   B. White Rose

   C. Green Rose

   D. Purple Rose

5. **Which of the following is a famous example of stained glass?**

   A. York Minster

   B. Bayeux

   C. Vindolanda

   D. Housestead

6. **During the Middle Ages, several cathedrals had windows of stained glass, telling stories about:**

   A. The journey of pilgrims to Canterbury

   B. Noah's Ark

   C. The Bible and Christian saints

   D. Medieval priests

7. **Daffodil is the national flower of Northern Ireland.**

   A. True

   B. False

8. **During the Middle Ages, great landowners and bishops sat in the House of Lords.**

    A. True

    B. False

9. **The Council of Europe has no power to make laws.**

    A. True

    B. False

10. **If the jury finds a defendant guilty, the judge decides the penalty.**

    A. True

    B. False

11. **Emmeline Pankhurst died in 1925.**

    A. True

    B. False

12. **The Mercury Music Prize is awarded each July for the best album from the UK and Ireland.**

    A. True

    B. False

13. **Which of the following statements is CORRECT?**

    A. The European Council is not the main part of the British government.

    B. The local government is not the main part of the British government.

14. **Which of the following statements is CORRECT?**

    A. 'The University Challenge' is an annual set of rowing races between the Cambridge University Boat Club and the Oxford University Boat Club.

    B. 'The Boat Race' is an annual set of rowing races between the Cambridge University Boat Club and the Oxford University Boat Club.

15. **Which of the following statements is CORRECT?**

    A. Europe's longest dry ski slope is located near Edinburgh.

    B. Europe's longest dry ski slope is located near Glasgow.

16. **Which of the following statements is CORRECT?**

    A. SW1A 0PW is the postcode of The House of Lords.

    B. SW2A 1PW is the postcode of The House of Lords.

17. **Which of the following statements is CORRECT?**

    A. David Allan was a Scottish painter who was best known for painting portraits. One of his most famous works is called'The Origin of Art'.

    B. David Allan was a Scottish painter who was best known for painting portraits. One of his most famous works is called'The Origin of Painting'.

18. **Which of the following statements is CORRECT?**

    A. St. David's Day is celebrated on March 1.

    B. St. David's Day is celebrated on March 21.

19. **Which of the following were famous British Novelists? (Choose TWO)**

    A. Jane Austen

    B. Victor Hugo

    C. Charles Dickens

    D. Dan Brown

20. **Which of the following countries fought alongside Britain against Russia during the Crimean War? (Choose TWO)**

    A. Cyprus

    B. Germany

    C. France

    D. Turkey

21. **In 1603, when Elizabeth I died her heir was her cousin James VI of Scotland who became King James I of: (Choose TWO)**

A. England

B. Scotland

C. Wales

D. None of above

22. **In the 2022 World Cup, England national football team drew the ___, ___ and Wales in Group B. (Choose TWO)**

A. USA

B. Iran

C. Netherlands

D. Iceland

23. **Which of the following buildings are located in London? (Choose TWO)**

A. The Shard

B. BT Tower

C. Greencastle

D. Tour Total

24. **24. Pubs are usually open from _____**

    A. 10.00am

    B. 11.00am

    C. 4.00pm

    D. 6.00pm

END OF THE TEST

Answers
答案及解題 (Mock Paper 1)

1. A

These settlements were known as plantations.

這些定居點被稱為種植園。

2. B

Dame Ellen MacArthur is a yachtswoman and in 2004 became the fastest person to sail around the world single-handed.

愛倫·麥克阿瑟夫人是一名帆船運動員，她於 2004 年成為單手環球航行速度最快的人。

3. B

One of the traditional characters of the pantomimes is the Dame, a female character played by a man.

Dame 是默劇入面較常出現的女性角色，通常會由男性扮演。

4. A

During the Wars of the Roses, the symbol of Lancaster was a red rose.

在玫瑰戰爭進行期間，紅玫瑰為蘭卡斯特的象徵。

5. A

York Minster is a famous example of stained glass used on the windows of some cathedrals during the middle ages.

在中世紀，一些大教堂會用上彩繪玻璃，其中約克大教堂就是一例。

6. C

During the Middle Ages, several cathedrals had windows of stained glass, telling stories about the Bible and Christian saints. The glass in York Minster is a famous example.

在中世紀，歐洲一些大教堂都有彩繪玻璃，來幫助講解聖經和基督教聖徒的故事，其中約克大教堂的彩繪玻璃就是一個著名例子。

7. B - False 錯誤

Daffodil is the national flower of Wales, while Shamrock is the flower associated with Northern Ireland.

水仙花是威爾斯的國花，至於三葉草則是北愛爾蘭的國花。

8. A - True 正確

During the Middle Ages, great landowners and bishops sat in the House of Lords.

在中世紀，大地主和主教坐在上議院。

9. A - True 正確

The Council of Europe has no power to make laws but draws up conventions and charters.

歐洲理事會雖無權立法，但仍可以制定公約和章程。

10. A - True 正確

If the jury finds a defendant guilty, the judge decides the penalty.

如果陪審團認為被告有罪，則法官決定刑罰。

11. B - False 錯誤

Emmeline Pankhurst died in 1928. Shortly before Emmeline's death, women were given the right to vote at the age of 21, the same as men.

艾米琳・潘克斯特於 1928 年去世。在她去世前不久，女性在 21 歲時獲得了與男性相同的投票權。

12. B - False 錯誤

The Mercury Music Prize is awarded each September for the best album from the UK and Ireland.

水星音樂獎每年 9 月頒發給來自英國和愛爾蘭的最佳專輯。

13. A

The European Council is not the main part of the British government.

歐洲理事會不是英國政府的主要組成部分。

14. B

The Boat Race is an annual set of rowing races between the Cambridge University Boat Club and the Oxford University Boat Club. It is the oldest inter-school rowing competition in the world.

牛津大學和劍橋大學之間每年都會在泰晤士河上合辦賽艇比賽，名為「牛津劍橋賽艇對抗賽」，那是世界上歷史最悠久的校際賽艇比賽。

15. A

Europe's longest dry ski slope is located near Edinburgh.

歐洲最長的旱雪場位於愛丁堡附近。

16. A

SW1A 0PW is the postcode of The House of Lords.

SW1A 0PW 是上議院的郵政編碼。

17. B

David Allan was a Scottish painter who was best known for painting portraits. One of his most famous works is called 'The Origin of Painting'.

大衛•亞倫是一位蘇格蘭畫家以畫肖像聞名。他最著名的作品之一是《繪畫的起源》。

18. A

St. David's Day is celebrated on March 1.

聖大衛節為每年 3 月 1 日。

19. A, C

Jane Austen and Charles Dickens were famous British Novelists.

珍•奧斯丁和查理•狄更斯是英國著名的小說家。

20. C, D

From 1853 to 1856, Britain fought with Turkey and France against Russia in the Crimean War.

英國於 1853 至 1856 年克里米亞戰爭中，與法國和土耳其一起對抗俄羅斯。

21. A, C

In 1603, when Elizabeth I died her heir was her cousin James VI of Scotland who became King James I of England and Wales.

1603 年，伊莉莎白一世去世時，她的繼承人是其堂兄：蘇格蘭的占士六世，占士六世後來成為英格蘭和威爾斯國王占士一世。

22. A, B

In the 2022 World Cup, England national football team drew the USA, Iran and Wales in Group B.

2022 年世界盃，英格蘭國家隊會和美國、伊朗和威爾斯同處B 組。

23. A, B

The Shard and the BT Tower are located in London

碎片大廈和英國電信塔都座落倫敦。

24.A

Pubs are usually open from 11.00am.

酒吧通常從上午 11 點開始營業。

3.2 Mock Paper 2

The test consists of 24 questions, and you need to answer at least 18 correctly to pass.

1. **Who is the head of the Church of England?**

    A. The Pope

    B. The monarch

    C. The Archbishop of Canterbury

    D. Prime Minister

2. **Who is responsible for maintaining relationships with foreign countries in government?**

    A. The Chancellor of the Exchequer

    B. The Foreign Secretary

    C. The Home Secretary

    D. The Queen

3. **Where did Mary Stuart, the Queen of Scotland, spend most of her childhood?**

    A. Spain

    B. Germany

    C. Holland

    D. France

4. **How many years did the war of a hundred years last for?**

   A. 100

   B. 101

   C. 115

   D. 116

5. **When did James Gordon Brown become Prime Minister?**

   A. 2007

   B. 2008

   C. 2009

   D. 2010

6. **Where in England was one of the Anglo-Saxon kings buried with treasure and armor?**

   A. Maiden Castle, Dorset

   B. Sutton Hoo, Suffolk

   C. Conwy Castle, Wales

   D. The Tower of London

7. **Patrick Steptoe invented the cash-dispensing ATM.**

   A. True

   B. False

8. **Anglo-Saxon was the most spoken language during the Iron Age.**

   A. True

   B. False

9. **The National Trust works for the preservation of important buildings, coastline and countryside in the UK.**

   A. True

   B. False

10. **On Christmas Day families traditionally sit down to a dinner of roast turkey and Christmas pudding, a rich steamed pudding made from suet, dried fruit and spices.**

    A. True

    B. False

11. **King Richard III was the first king of the House of Tudor.**

    A. True

    B. False

12. **Lewis Hamilton, Jenson Button and Damon Hill they are football players.**

    A. True

    B. False

13. **Which of the following statements is CORRECT?**

    A. Every year on Remembrance Day in the UK, people wear a red poppy.

    B. Every year on Remembrance Day in the UK, people wear a white poppy.

14. **Which of the following statements is CORRECT?**

    A. 'Old Bailey' is probably the most famous criminal court in the world.

    B. 'Old Trafford' is probably the most famous criminal court in the world.

15. **Which of the following statements is CORRECT?**

    A. 'Pinewood Studios Group' has a claim to being the oldest continuously working film studio facility in the world.

    B. 'Ealing Studios' has a claim to being the oldest continuously working film studio facility in the world.

16. **Which of the following statements is CORRECT?**

    A. In Northern Ireland, cases are heard by a District Judge or Deputy District Judge, who is legally qualified but unpaid.

    B. In Northern Ireland, cases are heard by a District Judge or Deputy District Judge, who is legally qualified and paid.

17. **Which of the following statements is CORRECT?**

    A. The West End of London is also known for 'Theatreland'.

    B. The West End of London is also known for rugby.

18. **Which of the following statements is CORRECT?**

    A. Henry VIII died on the 28th of January 1547.

    B. Henry VIII died on the 28th of January 1548.

19. **Which of the following languages were used across England during the Middle Ages? (Choose TWO)**

   A. Welsh

   B. Gaelic

   C. Norman French

   D. Anglo-Saxon

20. **Famous music festivals include Glastonbury, _____and _____.**

   A. the Isle of Wight Festival

   B. the V Festival

   C. the Bonnaroo Music and Arts Festival

   D. the Lollapalooza

21. **People in the UK have to pay tax on their income, which includes: (Choose TWO)**

   A. All ISAs and Savings Certificates

   B. Wages from paid employment

   C. Taxable benefits

   D. Pension Credit

22. **What should you do to make a complaint about the police? (Choose TWO)**

   A. Write a complaint letter to the House of Commons.

   B. Go to the Police station directly.

   C. Write to the Chief Constable of the police force involved

   D. Write to your MP

23. **Which of the following lines are from the National Anthem? (Choose TWO)**

   A. O say can you see, by the dawn's early light

   B. God save our gracious Queen

   C. Happy and glorious

   D. O say does that star-spangled banner yet wave

24. **Which of the following National Parks are located in England? (Choose TWO)**

   A. Southumberland

   B. Northumberland

   C. Old Forest

   D. Dartmoor

END OF THE TEST

Answers
答案及解題 (Mock Paper 2)

1. B

The monarch is the head of the Church of England.

君主是英格蘭教會的領袖。

2. B

The Foreign Secretary is responsible for managing relationships with foreign countries.

外交大臣主理與外國的關係。

3. D

Mary Stuart, the Queen of Scotland, spent most of her childhood in France.

蘇格蘭女王瑪麗・斯圖爾特的童年大部分時間都在法國度過。

4. D

English kings fought a long war with France, called the Hundred Years War (even though it actually lasted 116 years).

英國與法國曾打了一場歷時逾百年的漫長戰爭，史稱「百年戰爭」，但實際為 116 年。

5. A

Gordon Brown took over as Prime Minister from Tony Blair in 2007.

白高敦在 2007 年從貝理雅手中接任首相一職。

6. B

The burial place of one of the Anglo-Saxon kings was at Sutton Hoo in modern Suffolk.

該盎格魯-撒克遜國王的墓地位於現代薩福克郡的薩頓胡。

7. B - False 錯誤

In the 1960s, James Goodfellow invented the cash-dispensing ATM (automatic teller machine) or 'cashpoint'.

在 1960 年代，占士・古德費洛發明了自動取款機。

8. B - False 錯誤

The language spoken during the Iron Age was part of the Celtic language family.

鐵器時代使用的語言是凱爾特語系的一部分。

9. A - True 正確

The National Trust works for the preservation of important buildings, coastline and countryside in the UK.

國民信託致力於保護英國的重要建築、海岸線和鄉村。

10. A - True 正確

On Christmas Day families traditionally sit down to a dinner of roast turkey and Christmas pudding, a rich steamed pudding made from suet, dried fruit and spices.

在聖誕節，傳統上每個家庭都會坐下來享用烤火雞和聖誕布甸，這是一種由羊脂、乾果和香料製成的濃郁蒸布甸。

11. B - False 錯誤

Henry VII (Henry Tudor) was the first king of the House of Tudor.

亨利七世（Henry Tudor）是都鐸王朝的第一任國王。

12. B - False 錯誤

Lewis Hamilton, Jenson Button and Damon Hill have won the Formula 1 World Championship.

劉易斯‧漢密爾頓、簡森‧巴頓和達蒙‧希爾是賽車手，三位都分別贏得一級方程式賽車世界冠軍的殊榮。

13. A

That kind of red poppy flower was found on the battlefield of the First World War, so people used this flower to mourn the victims of the First World War.

該種紅色的虞美人花，曾於第一次世界大戰的戰場上發現，故後世用該種花，藉以悼念第一次世界大戰的死難者。

14. A

'Old Bailey' refers to The Central Criminal Court of London, England. Containing 19 courts and 70 prisoner cells.

「老貝利」指位於英國倫敦的中央刑事法院，法院入面包含 19 個法庭和 70 間囚室。

15. B

'Ealing Studios' has a claim to being the oldest continuously working film studio facility in the world.

伊靈工作室號稱是「世上最古老、且連續運作的」電影製片廠。

16. B

In Northern Ireland, cases are heard by a District Judge or Deputy District Judge, who is legally qualified and paid.

在北愛爾蘭，案件由具法律資格並獲薪酬的地區法官（或副地區法官）審理。

17. A

London's West End is one of the world's two major theater centers, as famous as Broadway in New York.

倫敦西區是與紐約百老匯齊名的世界兩大戲劇中心之一。

18. A

Henry VIII died on the 28th of January 1547.

亨利八世於 1547 年 1 月 28 日去世。

19. C, D

The Middle Ages saw the development of a national culture and identity. After the Norman Conquest, the king and his noblemen had spoken Norman French and the peasants had continued to speak Anglo-Saxon.

中世紀見證了民族文化和身份的發展。在諾曼征服之後，國王和他的貴族說諾曼法語，農民繼續說盎格魯-撒克遜語。

20. A, B

Famous music festivals include Glastonbury, the Isle of Wight Festival and the V Festival.

著名的音樂節包括格拉斯頓伯里音樂節、懷特島音樂節和維珍音樂節。

21. B, C

People in the UK have to pay tax on their income, which includes wages from paid employment and taxable benefits.

在英國，個人必須為其收入納稅，當中包括有償工作的薪金，以及應稅補貼。

22. B, C

Anyone can make a complaint about the police by going to a police station and writing to the Chief Constable of the police force involved. Complaints can also be made to an independent body: the Independent Police Complaints Commission in England and Wales, the Police Complaints Commissioner for Scotland or the Police Ombudsman for Northern Ireland.

任何人都可以通過前往警局，並寫信給警察局長投訴警員。此外，你亦可以向一些獨立機構作出申訴，例如英格蘭和威爾斯的「獨立警察投訴委員會」、蘇格蘭的警察投訴專員，又或者北愛爾蘭的警察監察員。

23. B, C

God save our gracious Queen and Happy and glorious are lines from the National Anthem.

God save our gracious Queen 和Happy and glorious 是英國國歌的歌詞。

24. B, D

National Parks in England: Broads / Dartmoor / Exmoor / Lake District / New Forest / Northumberland / North York Moors / Peak District / South Downs / Yorkshire Dales

英格蘭的國家公園有：布羅德斯國家公園 / 達特穆爾國家公園 / 埃克斯穆爾國家公園 / 湖區國家公園 / 新森林國家公園 / 諾森伯蘭國家公園 / 北約克沼澤國家公園 / 峰區國家公園 / 南唐斯國家公園 / 約克郡山谷國家公園

3.3 Mock Paper 3

The test consists of 24 questions, and you need to answer at least 18 correctly to pass.

1. **Which British writer wrote satirical novels including 'Brideshead Revisited'?**

   A. Evelyn Waugh

   B. Sir Arthur Conan Doyle

   C. Sir Kingsley Amis

   D. Thomas Hardy

2. **What marked the beginning of 'constitutional monarchy'?**

   A. The laws passed after the Glorious Revolution

   B. A speech given by the Queen

   C. The emergence of new ideas about politics, philosophy and science

   D. The development of the Bessemer process

3. **What was meant by the 'Divine Right of Kings'?**

   A. The idea that the kingdom was appointed by landowners

   B. The Parliament and the King shared responsibilities

   C. The King could rule the country but with the support of the Parliament

   D. The idea that the king was directly appointed by God to rule

4. **All dogs in public places must wear:**

   A. Collar with the name and address of the owner.

   B. Wellington boots

   C. Sunglasses

   D. Raincoat

5. **Which of the following is not the responsibility of the MPs?**

   A. Scrutinise and comment on what the government is doing

   B. Represent everyone in the constituency

   C. Protect life and property

   D. Debate important national issues

6. **When is the anniversary of the Battle of Boyne celebrated in North Ireland?**

   A. 3

   B. 5

   C. 6

   D. 7

7. **According to the 2011 census, 20% of British people said they had no religion.**

   A. True

   B. False

8. The people of the Iron Age had a sophisticated culture and economy. They made the first coins to be minted in Britain, some inscribed with the names of Iron Age kings.

A. True

B. False

9. 'The Festival of Lights' is another name given to Diwali.

A. True

B. False

10. When were women allowed to vote in 1928.

A. True

B. False

11. Maiden Castle is located in Somerset.

A. True

B. False

12. The Queen has important ceremonial roles, such as the opening of the new parliamentary session each year.

A. True

B. False

13. Which of the following statements is CORRECT?

A. There are five ski centers in Scotland.

B. There are eight ski centers in Scotland.

14. **Which of the following statements is CORRECT?**

   A. In 1801, Ireland became unified with England, Scotland and Wales after the Act of Union of 1800. This created the United Kingdom of Great Britain and Ireland.

   B. In 1802, Ireland became unified with England, Scotland and Wales after the Act of Union of 1800. This created the United Kingdom of Great Britain and Ireland.

15. **Which of the following statements is CORRECT?**

   A. Henry Purcell was an opera composer. He wrote church music, operas and other pieces, and developed a British style distinct from that elsewhere in Europe.

   B. Henry Purcell was the organist at Westminster Abbey. He wrote church music, operas and other pieces, and developed a British style distinct from that elsewhere in Europe.

16. **Which of the following statements is CORRECT?**

   A. 'Life peers' are appointed by the monarch on the advice of the Prime Minister.

   B. 'Life peers' are appointed By the Prime Minister on the advice of the monarch.

17. **Which of the following statements is CORRECT?**

   A. The Giant's Causeway is located on the south-west coast of Northern Ireland.

   B. The Giant's Causeway is located on the north-east coast of Northern Ireland.

18. **Which of the following statements is CORRECT?**

A. Lucian Freud was an important contributor to the 'pop art' movement of the 1960s and continues to be influential today.

B. David Hockney was an important contributor to the 'pop art' movement of the 1960s and continues to be influential today.

19. **Which of the following National Parks are located in Wales? (Choose TWO)**

A. Brecon Beacons

B. Snowdonia

C. Peak District

D. Yorkshire Dales

20. **Which of the following National Parks below are located in Scotland? (Choose TWO)**

A. Exmoor

B. South Downs

C. Cairngorms

D. Loch Lomond & The Trossachs

21. **If you are a dog owner, which of the following things should your dog's collar have when you go out for a walk? (Choose TWO)**

A. Owner's address

B. Owner's name

C. Dog's breed

D. Dog's name

22. **Which of the following issues can the devolved administrations pass laws on? (Choose TWO)**

    A. Defence

    B. Social security

    C. Health

    D. Education

23. **Which two of the following are Civil War Battles? (Choose TWO)**

    A. The Battle of Waterloo

    B. The Battle of Edgehill

    C. The Storming of Bristol

    D. The Battle of Agincourt

24. **Bradley Wiggins is a cyclist. In 2012, he became the first Briton to win the Tour de France. He has won seven Olympic medals, including gold medals in the 2004, _____ and _____ Olympic Games. (Choose TWO)**

    A. 2008

    B. 2012

    C. 2016

    D. 2020

END OF THE TEST

Answers
答案及解題 (Mock Paper 3)

1. A

Evelyn Waugh wrote satirical novels, including 'Decline and Fall' and 'Scoop'. She is perhaps best known for 'Brideshead Revisited'.

伊芙琳‧沃寫過多部諷刺小說，包括《衰落與墮落》和《獨家新聞》，但要數她最出名的作品，相信是《重返布萊茲海德莊園》了。

2. A

The laws passed after the Glorious Revolution are the beginning of what is called 'constitutional monarchy'.

於光榮革命後所通過的法律，是為君主立憲制的開端。

3. D

The 'Divine Right of Kings' refers to the idea that the king was directly appointed by God to rule and that the king should be able to act without having to seek approval from Parliament.

「皇權神授」是指國王由上帝直接任命，幫助管治國家的說法，是故國王應該能夠在沒徵得議會批准的情況下，行使權力。

4. A

All dogs in public places must wear a collar with the name and address of the owner.

在公共場所的狗隻，均須戴上寫有主人姓名和地址的項圈。

5. C

MPs have a number of different responsibilities. They represent everyone in their constituency, help to create new laws, scrutinize and comment on what the government is doing and debate important national issues.

國會議員有許多職責，他們是代表其選區中的每個人，幫助制定新法律、審查和評論政府正在做的事情，並就重要的國家問題進行辯論。

6. D

In N.Ireland, the anniversary of the Battle of the Boyne is celebrated in July.

北愛爾蘭的博因河戰役紀念日，定於每年 7 月慶祝。

7. B - False 錯誤

According to the 2011 census, 25% of people said they had no religion.

根據 2011 年人口普查，25% 的人表示自己沒有宗教信仰。

8. A - True 正確

The people of the Iron Age had a sophisticated culture and economy. They made the first coins to be minted in Britain, some inscribed with the names of Iron Age kings.

鐵器時代的人們擁有複雜的文化和經濟。他們鑄造了英國的第一批硬幣，有些硬幣上刻有鐵器時代國王的名字。

9. A - True 正確

The Festival of Lights, the religious celebration that celebrates the victory of good over evil and the gaining of knowledge.

燈光節是用以慶祝「善」戰勝「惡」，以及獲得知識的宗教慶典。

10. B - False 錯誤

In 1918 the Representation of the People Act was passed which allowed women over the age of 30 who met a property qualification to vote

英國政府在1918年通過了《人民代表法》，允許 30 歲以上符合資格的婦女投票。

11. B - False 錯誤

A very impressive hill fort can be seen today at Maiden Castle, in the English county of Dorset.

今天在英國多塞特郡的梅登城堡，你可以看到一個令人印象深刻的山堡。

12. A - True 正確

The Queen has important ceremonial roles, such as the opening of the new parliamentary session each year. On this occasion the Queen makes a speech which summarizes the government's policies for the year ahead.

英女王具有重要的禮儀角色，例如在每年新議會會議主持開幕儀式。活動上，女王會發表講話，講述政府未來一年的施政。

13. A

There are five ski centers in Scotland: CairnGorm Mountain, Glencoe Mountain, Glenshee, Nevis Range and The Lecht. Three of these are found in the Cairngorms National Park.

蘇格蘭有五個滑雪中心：凱恩戈姆山、格倫科山、葛蘭西、尼維斯山脈和萊希特。其中三個位於凱恩戈姆山國家公園。

14. A

In 1801, Ireland became unified with England, Scotland and Wales after the Act of Union of 1800. This created the United Kingdom of Great Britain and Ireland.

1801 年，愛爾蘭在 1800 年聯合法案後與英格蘭、蘇格蘭和威爾斯統一，從而創建「大不列顛及愛爾蘭聯合王國」。

15. B

Henry Purcell was the organist at Westminster Abbey. He wrote church music, operas and other pieces, and developed a British style distinct from that elsewhere in Europe.

亨利·珀塞爾是威斯敏斯特教堂的管風琴師，創作了教堂音樂、歌劇和其他作品，並發展出一種跟歐洲其他地方不同的獨特風格。

16. A

'Life peers' is a person who is given the honor of a title such as "Lord" and a place in the House of Lords as a reward for the good things they have done for the country. The honor is appointed by the monarch on the advice of the Prime Minister

被授予「終身貴族」稱號的人，會在上議院獲得一席，以作為其為國家所做的好事的獎勵。該銜頭是由君主根據首相的建議任命。

17. B

The Giant's Causeway is located on the north-east coast of Northern Ireland.

巨人堤道位於北愛爾蘭的東北海岸。

18. B

David Hockney was an important contributor to the 'pop art' movement of the 1960s and continues to be influential today.

大衛·霍克尼是 1960 年代「波普藝術運動」的重要推動者，至今仍具有影響力。

19. A, B

National Parks in Wales: Brecon Beacons / Pembrokeshire Coast / Snowdonia

威爾斯的國家公園有：布雷肯比肯斯國家公園 / 彭布羅克郡海岸國家公園 /
斯諾登尼亞國家公園

20. C, D

National Parks in Scotland: Cairngorms / Loch Lomond & The Trossachs

蘇格蘭的國家公園有：阿維莫爾凱恩戈姆國家公園 / 洛蒙德湖與特羅薩克斯
山國家公園

21. A, B

All dogs in public places must wear a collar showing the name and address of the
owner.

所有在公共場所的狗，都必須戴上寫有主人姓名和住址的頸圈。

22. C, D

Policy and laws governing defense, foreign affairs, immigration, taxation and social
security all remain under central UK government control. However, many other public
services, such as health and education, are controlled by the devolved administrations.

有關國防、外交事務、移民、稅收和社會保障的政策和法律均由英國中央政
府控制。然而，許多其他公共服務，如健康和教育，由下放的行政部門控制。

23. B, C

The Battle of Edgehill and The Storming of Bristol are Civil War Battles.

刀鋒山之戰和布里斯托爾風暴是英國兩場內戰

24. A, B

Bradley Wiggins is a cyclist. In 2012, he became the first Briton to win the Tour de
France. He has won seven Olympic medals, including gold medals in the 2004, 2008
and 2012 Olympic Games.

布拉德利・威金斯是一名自行車手。2012 年，他成為第一位贏得環法自行車
賽的英國人。他獲得了七枚奧運會獎牌，其中包括2004 年、2008 年和2012
年奧運會的金牌。

3.4 Mock Paper 4

The test consists of 24 questions, and you need to answer at least 18 correctly to pass.

1. **Who is responsible for crime, policing and immigration in the Cabinet?**

    A. Home Secretary

    B. Foreign Secretary

    C. Chancellor of the Exchequer

    D. Other Ministers

2. **When was Lincoln Cathedral built?**

    A. In the 19th century

    B. In mediaeval times

    C. After the Roman invasion

    D. In the 18th century

3. **How old was Edward VI (King Henry the 8th son) when he died?**

    A. 15

    B. 1

    C. 12

    D. 17

4. When was the Northern Ireland Assembly established?

A. Soon after the 1994 Belfast Agreement

B. Soon after the 1996 Belfast Agreement

C. Soon after the 1998 Belfast Agreement

D. Soon after the 2000 Belfast Agreement

5. St. Andrew is the Patron Saint of:

A. Scotland

B. Wales

C. England

D. Northern Ireland

6. Which of the following sentences is true?

A. The UK is governed by the parliament sitting in Edinburgh.

B. Scotland and Wales have parliaments or assemblies of their own, but not Northern Ireland.

C. Scotland, Wales and Northern Ireland also have parliaments or assemblies of their own, with devolved powers in defined areas.

D. The UK is governed by the parliament sitting in Glasgow.

7. **If you have a driving license from another country, you may use it in the UK for up to 2 years.**

   A. True

   B. False

8. **England, Scotland, Wales and Northern Ireland each have a guardian, collectively they are called 'the four guardian'. Each saint has a special day.**

   A. True

   B. False

9. **The Turing machine is a theoretical mathematical device invented by Alan Turing, a British mathematician, in the 1940s. The theory was influential in the development of computer science and the modern-day computer.**

   A. True

   B. False

10. **David Hume is an 18th century philosopher.**

    A. True

    B. False

11. **The Prime Minister appoints about 40 senior MPs to become ministers in charge of departments.**

A. True

B. False

12. **Hugh Grant has recently won an Oscar.**

A. True

B. False

13. **Which of the following statements is CORRECT?**

A. Lucian Freud was a German-born British artist. He is best known for his portraits.

B. Lucian Freud was a Britain-born German artist. He is best known for his portraits.

14. **Which of the following statements is CORRECT?**

A. Thomas Gainsborough was a portrait painter who often painted people in cities.

B. Thomas Gainsborough was a portrait painter who often painted people in country or garden scenery.

15. **Which of the following statements is CORRECT?**

    A. Ralph Vaughan Williams wrote music for orchestras and choirs. He was strongly influenced by traditional American folk music.

    B. Ralph Vaughan Williams wrote music for orchestras and choirs. He was strongly influenced by traditional English folk music.

16. **Which of the following statements is CORRECT?**

    A. Sir William Walton wrote a wide range of music, from film scores to opera. He wrote marches for the coronations of King George VI and Queen Elizabeth II but his best-known works are probably 'The Nutcracker', which became a ballet, and Balthazar's Feast, which is intended to be sung by a large choir.

    B. Sir William Walton wrote a wide range of music, from film scores to opera. He wrote marches for the coronations of King George VI and Queen Elizabeth II but his best-known works are probably Façade, which became a ballet, and Balthazar's Feast, which is intended to be sung by a large choir.

17. Which of the following statements is CORRECT?

   A. 'The Proms' is a six-week summer season of orchestral classical music.

   B. 'The Proms' is an eight-week summer season of orchestral classical music.

18. Which of the following statements is CORRECT?

   A. The NHS is the collective name for the four major public healthcare systems in the UK.

   B. The NHS is the collective name for the five major public healthcare systems in the UK.

19. British studios flourished in the 1930s. Eminent directors included _____ and _____, who later left for Hollywood and remained an important film director until his death in 1980. (Choose TWO)

   A. Sir Alexander Korda

   B. Steven Kings

   C. Charles Chaplin

   D. Sir Alfred Hitchcock

20. **Which two of the following records give us information about England during the reign of William I? (Choose TWO)**

A. The Magna Carta

B. The Domesday Book

C. The Bayeux Tapestry

D. The Canterbury Tales

21. **By law, which TWO types of media have to give a balanced coverage of all political parties and equal time to rival viewpoints before an election? (Choose TWO)**

A. Television

B. Internet

C. Newspapers

D. Radio

22. **Who can hear cases in Youth Courts in England, Wales and Northern Ireland? (Choose TWO)**

A. Specially trained magistrates

B. Social workers

C. District judges

D. Members of the public

23. **Early members of the Royal Society were: (Choose TWO)**

   A. Sir Edmund Halley

   B. Sir William Shakespeare

   C. Sir Isaac Newton

   D. Sir Geoffrey Chaucer

24. **Examples of criminal laws are: (Choose TWO)**

   A. Carrying a weapon or drugs

   B. Unfair dismissal or discrimination in the workplace

   C. Murder, racial crime

   D. None of the above

END OF THE TEST

Answers
答案及解題 (Mock Paper 4)

1. A

The Home Secretary is responsible for crime, policing and immigration in the Cabinet.

內政大臣負責處理治安和移民等事項。

2. B

Lincoln Cathedral was built in the middle ages.

林肯座堂建於中世紀。

3. A

Edward VI died at the age of 15 after ruling for just over six years, and his half-sister Mary became queen.

愛德華六世在位僅六年多後,於年僅 15 歲時就逝世了,其同父異母的妹妹瑪麗成為王后。

4. C

The Northern Ireland Assembly was established soon after the Belfast Agreement (or Good Friday Agreement) in 1998.

北愛爾蘭議會是在 1998 年貝爾法斯特協議(或聖週五協議)之後不久成立。

5. A

St. Andrew is the Patron Saint of Scotland.

聖安德魯為蘇格蘭的守護神。

6. C

Scotland, Wales and Northern Ireland also have parliaments or assemblies of their own, with devolved powers in defined areas.

蘇格蘭、威爾斯和北愛爾蘭都有各自的議會,並在特定領域下放權力。

7. B - False 錯誤

If you have a driving license from another country, you may use it in the UK for up to 12 months.

如果你擁有其他國家/ 地區的車牌，你可以在英國使用它長達 12 個月。

8. B - False 錯誤

England, Scotland, Wales and Northern Ireland each have a national saint, called a patron saint. Each saint has a special day.

英格蘭、蘇格蘭、威爾斯和北愛爾蘭各有一位國家聖人，稱為守護神。每個聖人都有一個特殊的日子。

1 March: St David's Day, Wales
17 March: St Patrick's Day, Northern Ireland
23 April: St George's Day, England
30 November: St Andrew's Day, Scotland

9. B - False 錯誤

The Turing machine was invented by Alan Turing in the 1930s.

「杜林機」是由亞倫・杜林，於 1930 年代發明。

10. A - True 正確

During the 18th century, the ideas of David Hume about human nature continue to influence philosophers.

在 18 世紀，大衛・休謨關於人性的觀點，一直影響著後來的哲學家。

11. B - False 錯誤

The Prime Minister appoints about 20 senior MPs to become ministers in charge of departments.

英國首相任命大約 20 名高級議員成為主管部門的部長。

12. B - False 錯誤

Recent British actors to have won Oscars include Colin Firth, Sir Antony Hopkins, Kate Winslet.

最近獲得奧斯卡獎的英國演員包括哥連費夫、安東尼鶴健士爵士和琦溫絲莉。

13. A

Lucian Freud was a German-born British artist. He is best known for his portraits.

盧西安・弗洛伊德是德國出生的英國藝術家。他最出名的是其肖像畫。

14. B

Thomas Gainsborough was a portrait painter who often painted people in country or garden scenery.

托馬斯・庚斯博羅是一位肖像畫家,經常在鄉村或花園風景中畫人物。

15. B

Ralph Vaughan Williams wrote music for orchestras and choirs. He was strongly influenced by traditional English folk music.

拉爾夫・沃恩・威廉姆斯為管弦樂隊和合唱團創作音樂。他深受傳統英國民間音樂的影響。

16. B

Sir William Walton wrote a wide range of music, from film scores to opera. He wrote marches for the coronations of King George VI and Queen Elizabeth II but his best-known works are probably Façade, which became a ballet, and Balthazar's Feast, which is intended to be sung by a large choir.

威廉・沃爾頓爵士創作了廣泛的音樂,從電影配樂到歌劇。他為喬治六世國王和伊莉莎白一世女王的加冕典禮寫了進行曲,但他最著名的作品可能是後來成為芭蕾舞劇的《門面》和打算由大型合唱團演唱的《伯沙撒王的盛宴》。

17. B

'The Proms' is an eight-week summer season of orchestral classical music. It takes place in various venues, including the Royal Albert Hall in London.

「逍遙音樂會」是一個為期八週的夏季管弦樂古典音樂季。音樂會在包括倫敦皇家阿爾伯特音樂廳在內的各個場所舉行。

18. A

The four public healthcare systems are:

四個公共醫療保健系統包括：

1. National Health Service 英格蘭國民保健署
2. Health and Social Care (Northern Ireland) 北愛爾蘭保健及社會服務署
3. NHS Scotland 蘇格蘭國民保健署
4. NHS Wales 威爾斯國民保健署

19. A, D

British studios flourished in the 1930s. Eminent directors included Sir Alexander Korda and Sir Alfred Hitchcock, who later left for Hollywood and remained an important film director until his death in 1980.

英國工作室在 1930 年代蓬勃發展。傑出的導演包括亞歷山大·科爾達爵士和阿爾弗雷德·希區柯克爵士，後者後來前往好萊塢並一直擔任重要的電影導演，直到 1980 年去世。

20. B, C

The Domesday Book and the Bayeux Tapestry give us information about England during the reign of William I.

《末日審判書》和巴約掛毯為我們提供了有關威廉一世統治時期英格蘭的信息。

21. A, D

By law, radio and television coverage of the political parties must be balanced and so equal time has to be given to rival viewpoints.

根據法律，電台廣播和電視報導必須在政黨作出平衡報道。

22. A, C

In England, Wales and Northern Ireland, if an accused person is aged 10 to 17, the case is normally heard in a Youth Court in front of up to three specially trained magistrates or a District Judge. The most serious cases will go to the Crown Court. The parents or carers of the young person are expected to attend the hearing. Members of the public are not allowed in Youth Courts, and the name or photographs of the accused young person cannot be published in newspapers or used by the media.

在英格蘭、威爾斯和北愛爾蘭，如果被告的年齡在 10 至 17 歲之間，案件通常在青年法庭由最多三名受過專門訓練的治安法官或一名地區法官審理。最嚴重的案件將提交刑事法庭。預計該年輕人的父母或照顧者將出席聽證會。公眾不得進入青少年法庭，被控青少年的姓名或照片不得在報紙上發表或被媒體使用。

23. A, C

Early members of the Royal Society were Sir Edmund Halley and Sir Isaac Newton.

皇家學會的早期成員是埃德蒙·哈雷爵士和艾薩克·牛頓爵士。

24. A, C

Examples of criminal laws are carrying a weapon or drugs and murder, racial crime.

刑事法的例子包括攜帶武器或毒品，以及謀殺和種族犯罪。

3.5 Mock Paper 5

The test consists of 24 questions, and you need to answer at least 18 correctly to pass.

1. **Which of the following lines from Shakespeare's plays and poems is often still quoted?**

   A. 'A daffodil by another name.'

   B. 'All the world's a stage.'

   C. 'We shall never surrender.'

   D. 'You shall be with me.'

2. **How many volunteers did the National Trust have when it first was formed in 1895?**

   A. 2

   B. 3

   C. 200

   D. 300

3. **In 1928 women in Britain received voting rights at the same age as men.**

   A. True

   B. False

4. **The Victoria Cross was introduced during:**

A. the First World War

B. the Second World War

C. the Boer War

D. the Crimean War

5. **What time do people hold a two minute silence on Remembrance Day?**

A. 9am

B. 10am

C. 11am

D. 12nn

6. **In 1200 the English ruled an area around Dublin, in _____, known as 'The Pale'.**

A. England

B. Scotland

C. Ireland

D. Wales

7. **The 'Concorde' began carrying passengers in the year of 1970.**

A. True

B. False

8. **Gilbert and Sullivan wrote the music for the popular show Jesus Christ Superstar.**

   A. True

   B. False

9. **The Prime Minister has control over many important public appointments.**

   A. True

   B. False

10. **Pantomimes are a British tradition that many theaters produce during Easter.**

    A. True

    B. False

11. **The first tennis club was founded in St Andrews in 1872.**

    A. True

    B. False

12. **The Northern Ireland Assembly building is known as Stormont and it is located in Dublin.**

    A. True

    B. False

13. **Which of the following statements is CORRECT?**

A. The present voting age of 18 was set in 1959.

B. The present voting age of 18 was set in 1969.

14. **Which of the following statements is CORRECT?**

A. The currency in the UK is the pound sterling ($).

B. The currency in the UK is the pound sterling (£).

15. **Which of the following statements is CORRECT?**

A. Henry VIII was king of England from 21 June 1497 until his death on 28 January 1547.

B. Henry VIII was king of England from 21 April 1509 until his death on 28 January 1547.

16. **Which of the following statements is CORRECT?**

A. Bodnant Garden is located in Northern Ireland.

B. Mount Stewart is located in Northern Ireland.

17. **Which of the following statements is CORRECT?**

A. The Mercury Music Prize is awarded each September for the best album from the UK and Ireland.

B. The Mercury Music Prize is awarded each October for the best album from the UK and Ireland.

18. **Which of the following statements is CORRECT?**

A. In the 1960s, Sir Peter Mansfield invented the Automatic Teller Machine (ATM).

B. In the 1960s, Scottish inventor James Goodfellow invented the Automatic Teller Machine (ATM).

19. **Examples of civil laws are: (Choose TWO)**

A. Carrying a weapon or drugs

B. Unfair dismissal or discrimination in the workplace

C. Murder, racial crime

D. Disputes between landlords and tenants

20. **New citizens _____ or _____ loyalty to the King as part of the citizenship ceremony. (Choose TWO)**

A. send

B. swear

C. affirm

D. sign

21. **The period after the Norman Conquest up until about 1485 is called: (Choose TWO)**

    A. The Age of Discovery

    B. The Middle Ages

    C. The Medieval period

    D. The Renaissance

22. **Which of the following territories does not belong to Great Britain?**

    A. England

    B. Wales

    C. Northern Ireland

    D. Scotland

23. **The 1950s and 1960s were a high point for British comedies, including Passport to Pimlico, _____and _____films. (Choose TWO)**

    A. The Ladykillers

    B. Carry On

    C. Marvel

    D. Lord of Rings

24. In the _____ and _____, a group called the Chartists campaigned for reform. They wanted six changes: for every man to have the vote, elections every year, for all regions to be equal in the electoral system, secret ballots, for any man to be able to stand as an MP and for MPs to be paid. (Choose TWO)

A. 1830s

B. 1840s

C. 1850s

D. 1860s

END OF THE TEST

Answers
答案及解題 (Mock Paper 5)

1. B

'All the world's a stage' is a line from William Shakespeare's play 'As You Like It'.

「全世界都是一個舞台。」是莎劇《如你所願》中的台詞。

2. B

The National Trust was founded in 1895 by three volunteers.

國民信託由三名志願者於 1895 年創立。

3. True 正確

1928 年，英國女性獲得與男性相同年齡的投票權。

4. D

the Crimean War 克里米亞戰爭

5. C

At 11am 於上午 11 時

6. C

In 1200 the English ruled an area around Dublin in Ireland, known as 'The Pale'

在 1200 年，英國人統治了都柏林周圍的愛爾蘭地區，後者又被稱為帕萊地區。

7. B - False 錯誤

The 'Concorde' began carrying passengers in the year of 1976.

和諧式客機於 1976 年開始用以接載乘客。

8. B - False 錯誤

Andrew Lloyd Webber has written the music for shows which have been popular throughout the world, including, in collaboration with Tim Rice, Jesus Christ Superstar and Evita, and also Cats and The Phantom of the Opera.

安德魯‧勞埃德‧韋伯為世界各地流行的節目創作了音樂，包括與蒂姆‧賴斯、耶穌基督巨星和艾薇塔，以及貓和歌劇魅影合作。

9. A - True 正確

The Prime Minister has control over many important public appointments.

首相掌管多個重要公職的人事任命。

10. B - False 錯誤

Many theaters produce a pantomime at Christmas time.

許多劇院在聖誕節期間製作默劇。

11. B - False 錯誤

The first tennis club was founded in Leamington Spa in 1872.

第一家網球俱樂部於 1872 年在皇家利明頓溫泉成立。

12. B - False 錯誤

The Northern Ireland Assembly building is known as Stormont and it is located in Belfast.

「北愛爾蘭議會大樓」又被稱為 Stormont，位於貝爾法斯特。

13. B

The present voting age of 18 was set in 1969.

目前 18 歲的法定投票年齡，是由 1969 年訂立。

14. B

The currency in the UK is the pound sterling (£).

英國的貨幣是英鎊（£）

15. B

Henry VIII was king of England from 21 April 1509 until his death on 28 January 1547.

英王亨利八世從 1509 年 4 月 21 日起坐上王位，直到他於 1547 年 1 月 28 日去世。

16. B

Mount Stewart is located in Northern Ireland, while Bodnant Garden is in Wales.

斯圖爾特山位於北愛爾蘭，至於博德南特花園則在威爾斯。

17. A

The Mercury Music Prize is awarded each September for the best album from the UK and Ireland.

水星音樂獎於每年 9 月舉行，獎項會頒給在英國和愛爾蘭推出的最佳專輯。

18. B

In the 1960s, Scottish inventor James Goodfellow invented the Automatic Teller Machine (ATM), and the first ATM was put into use by Barclays Bank in 1967.

蘇格蘭發明家占士・古德費洛在 1960 年代發明了自動提款機，而第一部自動櫃員機則在 1967 年於巴克萊銀行投入服務。

19. B, D

Examples of civil laws are unfair dismissal or discrimination in the workplace and disputes between landlords and tenants

民事法的例子有：在工作場所遭遇到不公平解僱或歧視，以及業主和租戶之間的糾紛。

20. B, C

New citizens swear or affirm loyalty to the King as part of the citizenship ceremony.

作為公民儀式的一部分，新公民須宣誓效忠國王。

21. B, C

The period after the Norman Conquest up until about 1485 is called the Middle Ages or the Medieval period.

在諾曼征服後，直到大約 1485 年的時期，被稱為「中世紀」或「中世紀時期」。

22. C

Great Britain' refers only to England, Scotland and Wales, not to Northern Ireland. The official name of the country is the United Kingdom of Great Britain and Northern Ireland.

大不列顛只指英格蘭、蘇格蘭和威爾斯，而不包括北愛爾蘭。英國的官方名稱是大不列顛及北愛爾蘭聯合王國

23. A, B

The 1950s and 1960s were a high point for British comedies, including Passport to Pimlico, The Ladykillers and Carry On films.

1950 年代和 1960 年代是英國喜劇的高潮，包括《Pimlico》、《The Ladykillers》和《Carry On》電影。

24. A, B

In the 1830s and 1840s, a group called the Chartists campaigned for reform. They wanted six changes: for every man to have the vote, elections every year, for all regions to be equal in the electoral system, secret ballots, for any man to be able to stand as an MP and for MPs to be paid.

在 1830 年代和 1840 年代，一個名為憲章派的團體提出改革運動。他們希望進行六項改變：每個人都有投票權，每年進行選舉，所有地區在選舉制度中平等，無記名投票，任何人都可以擔任國會議員，以及國會議員獲得報酬。

Chapter 4
常　見　問　題

1. **為什麼要參加和通過 Life in the UK Test ？**

   Life in the UK Test 是非常實用的英語語言和英國生活基本知識考核，從 2013 年 10 月 28 日起申請英國永居和入籍的所有人，除了18 歲以下以及65 歲以上，都必須通過這一考試，否則將功虧一簣，無法拿到永居簽證或入籍。

2. **英語不好，能不能通過 Life in the UK Test ？**

   Life in the UK Test 是一項入門級的英語語言測試，測試重點在英國的歷史、文化、政治和風俗習慣。任何人即使英語程度不是太好，只要通過有效地指導，針對性的訓練，絕對可以通過考試。

3. **代考或作弊是通過 Life in the UK Test 的辦法嗎 ？**

   絕對不能，經過 10 年多的運作，Life in the UK Test 的考試系統、監考方式和防止作弊方法已經完全成熟完備，幾年前的監考漏洞也已經完全堵塞。

   況且，一經發現代考或作弊，考試中心會立即報告移民局。在簽證政策如此緊縮的前提下，移民局會立刻備案，你此後遞交的任何簽證將不會被通過，甚至會在有效簽證到期後被拒絕再次入境一段長時間。

4. **除了簽證外，學習 Life in the UK Test 還有什麼好處？**

Life in the UK Test 不單是一項入門級的英語語言測試，更主要是對英國歷史、文化、政治和風俗習慣的瞭解和認知，對於你融入英國本地生活非常有效。

通過該考試的學習，你將對你決定定居或入籍的國家——英國——有一個簡單但全面的瞭解，明白這個國家的運行方式和系統，得知她的歷史和國家組成。

5. **英國政府對於 Life in the UK test 有指定教科書嗎?**

英國home office 有認可參考書籍《Life in the United Kingdom - A Guide for New Residents》，有需要朋友可以到英國大型書店，例如 Waterstones，又或網上購買。

6. **是不是在申請永久居留權之前，才可以報考Life in the UK test 呢？**

不是，只要你身在英國，就可報考Life in the UK test ，而且跟 IELTS 不同，沒有設定有效期，即是只要一經考試合格，終身有效。

7. **若果Life in the UK test 不合格，可以補考嗎？**

這個不是一試定生死，Life in the UK test 可以不限次數重考。

英國入籍試 解題天書 Life in the UK Test

作　　者：Koo Sir
責任編輯：麥少明
版面設計：吳國雄
出　　版：生活書房
電　　郵：livepublishing@ymail.com
發　　行：聯合新零售（香港）有限公司
地　　址：香港鰂魚涌英皇道1065號東達中心1304-06室
電　　話：（852）2963 5300
傳　　真：（852）2565 0919
初版日期：2022年11月
定　　價：HK$198 / NT$690
國際書號：978-988-75832-0-2
英國總經銷：Living Culture UK（電郵：LivingCulture@gmail.com）
台灣總經銷：貿騰發賣股份有限公司
電話： 02-8227 5988

網上購買 請登入以下網址：

一本 My Book One
www.mybookone.com.hk

香港書城 Hong Kong Book City
www.hkbookcity.com